# Dale Mayer

# the Haven

## BURKE 02

BURKE: THE HAVEN, BOOK 2
Beverly Dale Mayer
Valley Publishing Ltd.



ISBN-13: 978-1-778867-36-1
Print Edition

# Books in This Series:

Timber, Book 1
Burke, Book 2
Jaxon, Book 3

# About This Book

Burke, desperate for a fresh start, heads to Timber's place, hoping to exchange bed and board for some work around the refuge. He's trying to heal from a costly toxic relationship, but it seems the past isn't ready to let go. His ex has somehow secured credit cards in his name, determined to make him "pay" for the breakup.

The shocking details came to light when Shirley, his ex's sister, reaches out. She risks her own safety to warn him, putting herself on her sister's bad side—and, even worse, in the crosshairs of her sister's new boyfriend.

Amid the serenity of the Haven, Burke is caught in a whirlwind, trying to untangle this new mess while ensuring Shirley's safety. He's always had a soft spot for her. She is the shining light in that family, consistently proving her kindness and loyalty.

When the town becomes too dangerous for Shirley, Burke offers her refuge, knowing no one would dare trouble her here at the Haven. As they navigate these challenges together, a deepening bond begins to form between Burke and Shirley, a love that promises to heal old wounds and to offer a new beginning. Yet they both know she can't stay hidden forever …

**Sign up to be notified of all Dale's releases here!**
https://geni.us/DaleNews

AS TIMBER WOODLAND stepped outside, with the usual circle of happy dogs at his feet, a truck pulled in, and a man his age stepped out. Timber stared at him, confused for a moment. "Holy crap. *Burke?*"

Burke headed toward him, a big grin on his face. "I would give you a hug, but it looks as if you've got your hands full of—what is that, pancakes?"

Timber snorted, shoved the pancakes in his mouth, then reached out and grabbed Burke in an absolutely massive hug. "What the hell are you doing here?"

"I was talking to Badger and heard you'd gotten yourself into a big mess."

"Not so much now, but, honest to God, I feel as if I've just been released from a huge mess."

Burke nodded. "I heard that part too. Anyway, I'm kind of at loose ends, so I thought maybe … you could use a hand for a few days."

"Oh my God, I would absolutely freaking love it if you could stick around," Timber said. "We haven't had a chance to visit in a very long time."

"Not sure it'll happen now either. I've been told by more than a few people that you've got yourself a lady friend."

"Yeah, I do," he confirmed, with a beaming smile.

"Even with the leg?"

"Even with the leg, it doesn't seem to make a damn bit of difference to her."

"She's a veterinarian, I hear."

"She is a vet, and she's worked with Kat on some prosthetics for animals too."

"Dang, if she'd only seen me first," Burke boasted, "you would have been out of the running."

"I know. That's why I'm really glad that you didn't show up until now because she's already mine."

"Damn. She got a sister?"

"Nope, no sisters."

"How about a cousin?"

"I don't think so, but you can ask her tonight. She's coming for dinner."

At that, he slapped him on his head. "Man, I am so happy for you."

Timber smiled and nodded. "Thanks, buddy. It seems a long time coming."

"In so many areas," he agreed, "and I can't believe you've got all this."

"And so much more," he murmured. "It'll be a massive, massive sanctuary for animals."

"And what kind of animals have you got?"

"Oh, a few you may not expect," he replied, with a smile, "but that's okay because that's what a refuge is all about. It's a home for all. It's a safe haven."

"And is it just for four-legged animals?" he asked, his tone a little off as he looked at his friend.

"It can also be for two-legged animals," Timber stated, with a wry smile, "particularly ones in need."

"Yeah, I was kind of hoping you would say that. You got a place where I could bunk for a day or two?"

"Sure do," he replied, looking over at him. "Troubled

times?"

"Not so much troubled times, just maybe time for a rest."

"That's good enough for me," Timber said. "You know you've always got a home wherever I am."

"Thanks for that, man. I really needed to hear it." And, with that, the two men stood on the front porch, enjoying the bright sunshine. The dogs stretched out happily in front of them, Dodger sitting contentedly on the railing close by. Birds trilled and flew by, cutting through the trees.

Timber looked out and smiled. "It really is a brand-new day."

"Amen to that," Burke replied. "I could use a whole new day."

"And if you need a hand with something …"

"Maybe, … I've got to work my way through it first."

"Good enough. I won't push."

"Yeah, you will," Burke countered, a knowing smile on his face. "Just don't do it today." And, with that, he slapped him on the shoulder and added, "I heard there's work to be done."

"Yeah, there's plenty of that."

"And you pay in grub." Then, laughing and joking, they headed out to join the rest of the men who were already swinging hammers in the wind.

Timber never thought he would see anything quite so fine. So he picked up a hammer and joined them, a smile on his face and his heart full. His life had never looked quite so good. This place, aptly named the Haven, wasn't just for him, but for everybody else just like him, and that was even better.

From a short distance away, a doe with a spotted fawn by her side looked on, happily grazing.

# CHAPTER 1

SEVERAL WEEKS LATER Burke Thomas sipped his coffee on the deck as he watched the sunrise. Thankfully this arrangement had worked out for both him and Timber's massive log house. Dodger, the ever-faithful squirrel that had adopted Timber and now Burke, sat on the railing nearby, working on a peanut Burke had placed there. He smiled, reached out a finger, and stroked the squirrel's back, which didn't seem to faze him one bit. At this point in time, it seemed as if Dodger was more comfortable being hand-fed than foraging on his own. Hearing footsteps behind him in the kitchen, Burke looked up to see Timber stepping out onto the deck beside him.

He glanced down, smiled at Dodger, then reached up and stretched.

"Had a good night?" Burke asked him.

Timber nodded. "It was pretty decent. I have to admit, nothing like a day full of physical work to give you the need for a good solid rest at night."

"Agreed. Still, even knowing how many men you have here, I can't believe how fast some of this is going up."

"True, the basic structures are going up quickly, but a ton of finishing work will be left to be done, and you know how time-consuming that can be." He placed his hands on his hips, did a few more stretches, then walked over to the top of the steps. He stared out at the newly constructed bunkhouse, specifically for any long-term ranch hands. "That bunkhouse has a roof and four walls, but that's it."

In the meantime, Kat had shipped out here some smaller temporary units for sleeping quarters, some of which might remain for the more transient helpers who passed through the Haven. Now those residents had a communal space with multiple bathrooms and a kitchenette. A laundry unit at the back was currently in progress.

"And yet, what have you got, six guys sleeping in the unfinished bunkhouse?" Burke asked, with a laugh.

Timber glanced at him and nodded. "Hard to believe, isn't it?"

"It's a great thing though. You're doing a lot of good here, man."

"I started this for animals like Dodger," he noted, with a laugh. As Little Toby came out, wagging his tail, Timber bent down and scrubbed his ears and smiled at the dog.

"How many dogs are you aiming for?" Burke asked.

"I have five of my own, and that will be it for a while. With the other dogs that belong to the crew, all of them can be a bit much when they're loose like this all the time. Little Toby here belongs to Big Toby."

"Oh, right. And didn't Tiffany bring home another one?"

"She did, but he needs medical care and to get his strength back. As soon as he's healthy enough, he'll get a pen in the back, and we'll probably have one or two others with him, who are also medical rescues," he added, with a smile.

"Imagine you hooking up with a vet."

"I don't know about the *hooking up* part, but she's definitely a partner in this operation," he clarified, with a wave of his hand. Then he chuckled. "Badger and Kat have a fair share in it too."

"Is all the paperwork done for the new parcel of land yet?"

"Nope, … not yet. The lawyers are still working on it," he noted, with a smile, "but we have a contract. Now it's just a matter of finishing off the details."

"What about water on the new place?"

"There is a small lake and potentially a second one, with an underground spring," he shared. "So I'm hoping that would be a huge boon."

"And when you say a small lake …"

"Yeah, … I think it's stretched out over eight acres or so."

"That's hardly small."

"It's enough, and it will have its own ecosystem of wildlife. I'll get over there eventually and will figure out how to get that parcel fenced in," he muttered, with a groan. "It was quite a job to fence what we have now."

"I can imagine," Burke agreed, a bit envious.

"You're right though. It was great having all those guys out here to help us over the initial hump of development, and to buy that much more land is huge," he admitted.

"It is, but everything you're doing is for the right reasons, so I have no doubt that it will all end up in a good way."

Timber laughed. "I'm not a naysayer, and I definitely work on positive thinking," he explained, "but sometimes you just have to let go and to let life happen, then see how the cookie crumbles."

"That's one way to look at it."

When a shout came from inside, Timber turned around

and then told Burke, "That'll be Dwight, so breakfast is probably up."

"I'll go tell the guys at the bunkhouse."

But before he could make a move, the bunkhouse door opened, and men made their way toward them. Burke laughed. "These guys don't miss much, do they?"

"They never miss a meal, especially with Dwight and Toby cooking."

"Yeah, you sure lucked out with your cooks."

"I did, indeed—not what I was expecting either." Timber looked back and shrugged.

Burke asked, "Was Dwight supposed to be here for only a few days?"

"Yeah, just like a bunch of the other guys," Timber confirmed, with a big smile. "I'm so grateful for anybody who is working here, especially since none of them are getting paid," he muttered, shaking his head. "That's just amazing."

"But most of them are here because either they physically need to test out their prosthetics or need to psychologically be here helping others. One way or another they want to help out, or maybe this place is providing them with something they didn't have before."

"Sometimes all of the above," Toby interjected, as he stepped out on the deck and looked around to confirm people were coming.

Timber nodded. "You can never discount the benefit of what this place means to each individual person, nor their reasons for being here," Timber stated. "We all have our own reasons, and some of them are even good ones." And, with a good chuckle, he called out, "You guys better come inside. Dwight frets if no one eats his cooking."

Burke joined Timber as they headed into the kitchen,

grabbing plates and loading up generous servings of bacon and eggs, hash browns, and toast, with some waffles on the side.

"How the hell did you make waffles?" Timber asked Dwight.

"Kat sent over a waffle iron via Tiffany. Waffles are pretty damn easy to make, and sometimes a little variety is good," he muttered. "They're also pretty fast, and, when you feed gangs of men like we do here, anything that's fast works for me."

"If you need anything else, just let me know."

"Yeah, don't worry. I've already got a list going that I need to hassle you about."

"Great," Timber muttered. "Are we getting more deliveries?"

"I don't know if you've paid for the last one," he noted, with a smirk, "but, as soon as you have, you can bet that we'll need more, … yes."

"Right, I've got to get to the office and start paying some of those bills." Timber shook his head. "I get caught up in the work out here, and it's so easy to forget about the office work."

"Oh, you can't forget about that," Burke declared. "Once the money stops flowing, the supplies do too."

Timber smiled and nodded. "I hear you there. I'll get at it first thing this morning."

"Good enough," Dwight said, "and, yeah, we do need more supplies."

"Anything major? Do I need to go into town and get anything?"

"No, I spoke to Tiffany last night, and she'll bring some of it out with her tonight." When Timber frowned at that,

Dwight shook his head and asked, "What do you want me to say? She's coming here anyway and doesn't mind bringing stuff, as long as it's ready for her to pick up. Plus, they load it for her. That way it's not putting her out much. Plus, it's on her way," Dwight added, his gaze speaking volumes, "so it's even easier."

"I know," Timber muttered, but disquiet filled his tone.

Dwight looked at him, serious now, and added, "If you've got a problem with that, you better talk to her because you know as well as I do how she feels about you not letting her help."

Timber raised both hands in frustration. "She already does a lot."

"Of course she does, but not only does she want to help, that woman loves you, you moron," Dwight declared, with a snort. "You would think, after all this time, you would stop being an ass about it. Keep this up, and she'll realize you're a lost cause."

"Really?" Burke asked, with a laugh. "A lost cause for her or for Timber?"

"Both," Dwight muttered, with a headshake. "Now hurry up and eat. You guys got work to do."

"Yeah, that's true enough," Burke agreed. "We do have plenty of work to do."

WITH A SIGH Timber gave Little Toby another scratch and a piece of bacon, hiding it so Big Toby wouldn't see. Yet Big Toby saw it all and grumbled. Timber noted, "Little Toby still needs to fatten up a bit."

"On bacon?" Big Toby asked.

"Sure, why not?" Timber asked, with a laugh. After finishing his own breakfast, he got up and made way for a couple guys who were still coming in from the bunkhouse. He said good morning to all of them with a bright smile.

When they sniffed the waffles, they beelined for them.

Timber lifted a hand in a wave to all. "I'll head to the office first and get after those bills then, I guess."

"Good idea," Dwight agreed. "We need more grub."

Timber shook his head at that because it seemed as if nothing but groceries were brought into the house. Having lived alone for as long as he had, it was still a shock to see just how much was required to feed everybody. He would never argue about it though, especially since their labor was free. The price was right, and these guys were a godsend right now, and that was all Timber needed. It was enough to know that these men were well-fed and looked after while they were here, helping him.

As he stepped into one of the rooms in his cabin, now designated as his office, his cell phone rang, and he looked down with a smile to see it was Tiffany. "Good morning," he greeted her. "It sure would be nice if you lived here full-time."

"So you've mentioned," she quipped, followed by a laugh, "a few times."

"But you keep ignoring me."

"I'm not ignoring you," she stated, "but, for the moment, it's not exactly a doable idea."

"Sure, it is," he muttered, with a groan. "You spend nights here anyway."

"I spend *some* nights there," she clarified, correcting him. "So I don't spend every night there, and, while being there is a lovely prospect, I just don't want to push our relationship to the point that we jump into anything."

"We're hardly jumping into anything, but I hear you," he grumbled, "so I'll give you a little more time."

"*Gee, thanks,*" she replied in a teasing voice.

He groaned in response, but a smile still popped up on his face. He looked up to see Burke stopping in the doorway.

Burke apologized for interrupting. "Hey, I need to help the men, but I hear from Toby you'll be out tonight, right, Tiffany?"

"Yeah, I'll talk to him about picking up the supplies and confirm he's got everything ordered and waiting on me by then."

"Good enough. See you later."

And, with that, Timber disconnected and looked over at Burke.

"Can't get her to stay here?" Burke asked.

"Not full-time anyway," he replied, "but it won't be long."

"No, it won't, and you're lucky you've got her."

"I am," he agreed. "Any problem?"

"No, but the guys were just wondering how you wanted to organize the day."

"Right," he noted. "I'm coming."

"They were about to head out and continue the work assignments from yesterday, but I thought you told me there would be a change in plans."

"Yeah," he said, with a sigh, "that was the thought process, but I'll see how it goes." Timber and Burke headed out via the kitchen.

"It will probably go as well as you want it to," Dwight interjected, having overheard most of their conversation. "As long as Tiffany is picking up groceries and coming out again tonight, no reason to change very much, is there?”

“No, she isn’t involved in any of the work-schedule changes anyway,” Timber noted.

Big Toby shook his head. “Except that her clinic will be in the works on the property too. So, you’ll need to get her input on any changes in the design.”

“Some changes, but thankfully not a ton, as she had a lot of input in the initial planning. We have lots of framers right now, so we’re trying to take advantage of that and get as many of the structures up as we can. I was thinking we would do the other work as money, time, and the requisite skills came along,” he shared. “I know that sounds like a strange way to run a business but—”

“It’s not a business though, is it?” Burke asked.

“It’s a passion,” interjected Jaxon, as he joined them, a cup of coffee in hand. “Getting the structures up so other trades can take over is huge.”

Timber nodded. “I know a lot of people look at this and wonder what I’m up to, but I never really gave a shit what anybody else thought before, so not planning on starting now.” As all the men were grabbing coffee, Timber announced, “Okay, let’s sit down and get our plans going for the morning.” And, with that, he lined up what the next stages of each project would be, with everybody adding in their suggestions. When done, the men got up to head out to their designated spots for today’s projects.

Timber smiled at Toby and Dwight, finally seated and having their own breakfasts. Timber asked them, “What do you think?”

“I think it’s coming along great,” Dwight declared. “You’ve got a way to go on some of it, but you’re a hell of a lot farther along than I ever could have imagined at this point in time. It's been amazing."

"It has been, hasn't it?" Timber asked, with a grin. "We've still got some of the men Badger sent our way."

"Yep." Dwight nodded. "Plus, you've got Burke here for anything else you need done."

"I can give you a hand on some of the electrical," Toby offered, pushing back his plate, "which I guess you're close to needing next, aren't you?"

"Since the foundation and the framing are all set up in the bunkhouse already, we're just finishing off the small inner areas. We need the bathrooms and the lighting done in there, for sure."

"Okay, so I'll go work on the electrical today," Big Toby confirmed.

"You need any help with that?" Burke asked.

"If you're okay to let me have Sam, I'll pull him in to help me. He was an apprentice electrician, and he's damn good," Toby stated.

Burke added, "I think we should help that kid get back into trade school again."

"Is that what he wants to do?" Timber asked.

Burke nodded. "I think so, but he just figured he wouldn't be able to."

"Why not?" Timber asked.

"Because he's got a prosthetic," Burke muttered, looking at him.

When Timber frowned, Toby shrugged behind him. "We both know how that works, and, if it's not fully functioning, we tend to think it's a huge handicap—until we figure out that it's not."

"If the problem is the prosthetic itself, we should hook him up with Kat. If the problem is more about Sam's mind-set, that's something different. So will his injury be a handicap for him?" Timber asked, staring from Burke to Toby, then glancing over at Dwight.

"I don't think so," Toby declared, with a shrug. "Honestly, he's doing just fine."

"What do you want me to do?" Timber asked them, serious now.

Burke suggested, "Outside of having Kat check over Sam's prosthetic, do we know any electricians in town who could take him in on a part-time basis?"

Timber nodded. "I can find out and give it a shot. Toby, do you know how Sam feels about it? If he wants to go back to school?"

"I don't know," Toby admitted, "but I'll see if I can find out."

"Okay." Timber nodded. "I'll sniff around and see if we have any prospects. I'm starting to have a little pull around here, just not a whole lot," he noted, with a laugh, "but that's not an issue. We'll see what we can get to help out Sam."

With that, Toby grabbed his work belt off the hook by the door and announced, "I'll be working in the bunkhouse today, if you need me." With that, he headed off.

Timber turned to Burke. "And what about you?"

"I can work over there too, or I thought maybe I could get some of the basic plumbing done at the medical clinic in those intake rooms."

Timber frowned at that. "I forgot that you had a lot of plumbing experience."

"Yeah, I do, and you've already got a great septic system, which is a huge boon, but we'll have to run a few more pipes before that addition gets poured."

"Right, we'll need to expand that too, based on Tiffany's input." He winced. "That'll be a huge project. Yet it's definitely the right thing to do, but getting there all at once wasn't what I expected."

Burke shook his head at that. "I know. Getting there will be expensive, but you'll still be way better off in the end."

"I agree." Timber smiled. "No doubt it's the right thing to do, it's just …"

"You mean, it's the right thing to do, and, if it was somebody else's money, it would be a whole lot easier to agree to it."

Timber laughed.

"And yet, you're loving it. I know that you absolutely love having that medical center here."

"I do," Timber conceded. "It'll probably be my favorite building of all, but this has all moved a lot faster than what I imagined. And keeping on top of the to-do list, the expenses, and the timeline for each project is a huge headache."

"Of course," Burke agreed, with a smile, "and yet it's part and parcel to creating the Haven right here, coming into reality."

With that, the two of them headed toward the medical center and got to work. A lot of plumbing work had to be laid out, setting in big sinks for washing animals and additional sinks for the surgical sites. Two surgery rooms would be in here.

"You'll need somebody to help Tiffany too, you know?" Burke pointed out.

"What do you mean?" Timber asked, turning to him.

"If she's planning on doing surgeries here, and presumably moving her business here, she'll need an assistant, if this will be a full-time deal."

"I hadn't thought about that. I think she was thinking more along the lines of it being full-time because there would be enough animals here to supplement those in her existing practice, which *would* make it full-time," he muttered. "It seems foolish to consider right now, but you're correct. It could get very busy, very quickly."

"I think it'll get busy as soon as you get the word out that you're open for business, and I suspect that you're trying to hold that off as long as you can."

"I am," he confirmed, "because you're so right. As soon as anybody knows my place is open for business, it'll get a little chaotic, and we're not set up for it yet. We've got a bunch of dogs, and that's all good and easy, but …"

"And the horses?"

"Sure, we've got Andy's horses now, and we've got Danny the donkey," he added, with a smile, "and they're all staying. They'll be lifers here. Now that we also have acreage for quite a few more horses, we've contacted some of the local rescues. We'll be offering land, at least on a temporary basis, until some of the animals have other homes or get other locations they can be moved to."

"I never thought of that. I guess that's an important thing too, isn't it?"

"It is, as not everybody has space for them, but that is something I can now offer," he stated, with a smile. "We've got several acres over here in pasture now, and we'll have a lot more."

Just then his phone rang, and he looked at it and smiled. "This is somebody I was talking to the other day. I've got to take this." Then he turned and stepped off to the side.

Burke heard the conversation, but he continued working on the list of supplies needed for this job that he was taking on. He thought about everything that Timber was building and the size and the scope and how quickly it had enlarged, and Burke realized just how much life could be like that for him as well.

You take one step forward, and, all of a sudden, it's seventeen steps to the left that you hadn't really expected. Yet it would probably bring on a passionate outpouring for Timber and his rescue, the Haven. Burke hoped Timber had enough money to handle it because this was starting to take on a life of its own.

Burke was buried in water lines when Timber returned to help him out. "Everything okay?" Burke asked.

"Yeah, but we've got more horses coming, apparently fourteen of them."

"Fourteen?" Burke repeated.

Timber nodded at him. "These are seizures from a local rancher, and the nearby animal rehab facility is hoping to move out some of the animals, but the intake needs to happen soon. They can support a bunch of the horses, but they need to bring some of them to a place that's got space. So, they were talking to me and then checked in with Tiffany to confirm I was a viable option. She apparently gave us a clean bill of health, so they'll be coming sometime this afternoon."

"Fourteen horses though? Good God," Burke muttered. "As I said, this acreage will fill up quickly."

"This won't be permanent for these fourteen, but I hear you," Timber agreed, with a smile. "Then we have to consider whether all fourteen horses can be kept together in one area or if we need to separate some of them."

"Right, and what about stallions?"

"Hopefully there aren't any," Timber stated, "but, if

there are, each will need his own pen."

With that, the discussion continued for a while. Then they fell silent, as they got deeper and deeper into the physical work.

When they were finally done laying all the plumbing pipes and connecting them and making sure none leaked, Timber sat back with a big smile and declared, "Just in time."

"Only if we can get these sinks connected today. Do you have them here?" Burke asked. Timber pointed out the large boxes off to the side. Burke turned around and nodded. "Perfect, that can be the work for this afternoon," Burke said.

Timber frowned. "If we can get all the sinks and the faucets up and running, that would be huge."

"Except you've got animals coming this afternoon."

"Hopefully we won't have to do an awful lot for the horses, but if we do? … We just do," he stated, with a smile. "You've got lots of experience with horses, don't you?"

He shrugged. "I've got some, but it's been a while."

"That's fine. I just need people who are comfortable around them."

"Oh, I'm definitely comfortable around them," Burke added, "and, most of the time, they like me too."

Hearing a bark, both men turned to see Little Toby and another one of the new dogs, Max, at the doorway, both barking at whatever was happening in the front yard.

When Max had arrived, the men wanted to change his name immediately, since obviously there was residual animosity toward Max Killerman—a rogue veteran and the son of Andy, the rancher who had sold Timber the land. That Max had made life a living hell at the Haven, ultimately kidnapping Tiffany to torment Timber. Max was ultimately shot and killed in a standoff.

At the end of the day, they decided changing the dog's name would have confused him, so they decided against it.

Timber got up, took a look outside, and then whistled. Burke was unpacking and sorting the boxes of supplies designated for this building, but he froze when he turned to see a bobcat slink inside the door.

"It's okay," Timber muttered quietly. "This is Billy Bob. Just stay calm and don't make any sudden movements."

"Billy Bob? That's a hell of a name for a bobcat."

"Yeah. Hey, nobody ever said I was original."

Burke added, "You mentioned the other day that you saw him again, but I didn't expect him to get in so close and personal with us." As he continued to watch their visitor, the bobcat just stared at him, unblinking. "So, … is he thinking I'm his next meal or is he looking at me and wondering what the hell I'm doing here?"

"It could be both," Timber noted cheerfully. Then he laughed at the look on Burke's face. "Don't worry. Billy Bob's fairly well-fed, and he hunts on his own, which is a good thing. However, that just brings up another issue, considering I run a rescue and have some animals he might want to catch and eat."

"Yeah, like Dodger."

"That squirrel's probably too small for Billy Bob to bother with. If he was really hungry, … maybe he would trap a squirrel, but, then again, he is just a cat. A giant one at that, but still a cat. And we have to understand that he lives his life the same as anybody does."

"Got it," Burke noted, as he watched the bobcat, now stationed under the window, still staring at him. "Can you pet him?"

"Billy Bob? Oh, absolutely," Timber shared, with a smile, as he walked over and crouched in front of the bobcat. Immediately the cat turned into a big purring engine, walked over a few steps closer to Timber, and almost fell against his hands and his legs, rubbing up against him.

Burke gave a soft whistle. "That's not what I was expecting when it came to the animals here."

"I know, but what was I supposed to do? He had an injured tail and a nail sticking through his paw. It took a little bit to get close enough to treat him, but, once we were there," Timber said, "he's been a grateful soul ever since."

"And he sticks around," Burke muttered, as he continued to stare at the bobcat.

"He does, sometimes a little more than others, and lots of times he's just here for the ride and wants to keep us company," he stated, with a smile. "He and the dogs have to work things out once in a while, but it seems to be going okay."

"Unbelievable." As Burke bent to duck back under the sink to connect some pipes, he added, "I'll need a hand to get this into the wall over here." After installing the stainless-steel counter along the side with the sink at the front, they had that one treatment room finally fixed up. Burke stepped back and smiled. "How about that?"

"Good. Now we do it eight more times," Timber noted, with a sigh.

"Eight?"

"Not eight more treatment rooms, but eight more sinks with a similar layout. Some are just a little more extensive, as those rooms will be set up for animals that need long-term care, animals that we'll need to keep a little bit longer than normal, and we don't necessarily want them in cages."

"Right," Burke muttered. "Obviously I have a lot to learn, but I'll have fun watching you."

"Hey, you can stay as long as you want, particularly when you're giving me all this free labor."

"Not so much free labor, as you're giving me a place and a purpose right now," he clarified.

"It's a weird combination," Timber admitted, a smile playing on his lips. "Yet somehow it does seem to be working for people."

Burke looked over at him and smiled.

"Of course some people are probably hiding out here," Timber casually commented.

Burke stilled, then turned to face him. "Was that directed at me?"

Timber narrowed his gaze. "If need be, it can be."

Burke snorted at that. "I'm not hiding from anything," he declared, "but that's not the same thing as avoiding something, and *that* I'm doing. I am definitely *avoiding*."

"It's your business," Timber replied. "Anytime you want to talk, I'm here, but I'm not trying to pry."

"You might not be trying to pry, but there is definitely a sense of … something going on here that I hadn't really expected."

"And what is that?"

"A sense of community, a sense of purpose, a family maybe? A commonality of why everybody is here," he noted, with a smile. "That's not what I was expecting."

"Whatever it is, it happened naturally. I'm only here setting up a refuge for animals, and I hadn't even determined what animals and or how any of it would work. I figured I would be building it all myself, but somehow things snow-balled."

"I can see that, and, in your case, the snowballing was probably a good thing."

"Sure, but it still needs managing, and somehow I have to keep directing it to flow in the right direction"—he laughed—"and that's not necessarily an easy thing."

"No, but I don't think it's a hard thing either," Burke declared, looking over at him. "You've doing a great job."

Timber smiled, straightened up, and announced, "Okay, this room's done."

As Burke stood back to look at the finished treatment room, he pointed to the window. "I see Billy Bob left."

Timber came up behind him and nodded. "Time for a lunch break."

"Thank God for that." Burke groaned, straightening up again. He stood for a moment, waiting for the pain in his leg to settle.

"Leg that bad?"

"Just because I was in a weird position."

"And you'll take it easy, right?" Timber asked, his voice deep, his tone darkened with concern.

"Of course," he said, smiling over at his buddy.

Timber studied his friend and murmured, "If I can do anything to give you a hand, just let me know."

"Yeah, I hear you, but, unless you'll bring out a masseuse or install a hot tub," he shared, "I don't really think anybody can do anything."

"Sometimes just getting out and getting busy working on something else is a good help."

"Yeah, I've been focusing on that," he agreed, with a smile, "and it's doing great things for the mental health, but it's a little rough on the physical side."

"Some good fitness trainers and physiotherapists are in

town, depending on what you need, even some new people I hadn't seen before too," Timber shared.

"You checked them out?"

"I only went because Tiffany was talking about how this guy and his assistant were quite something. I don't understand it, or even know how to explain it, but they do some kind of energy work on the muscles. Something about engaging the muscles, turning off the right ones and turning on the *other* right ones," he explained, followed by a laugh. "Anyway, it's made a difference for me."

"Oh good." Burke frowned at him. "Sometimes you think nothing else can be done, and then, all of a sudden, somebody mentions, *Oh, have you tried this?* So maybe I'll make a trip into town to see those energy workers."

"If you want, I can set you up with an appointment with them. I don't know what their schedule is like, but I'm pretty sure they're busy."

"Of course they're busy." Burke sighed. "Seems as if anybody who's any good is busy. That's the way of it."

The two of them walked back toward the kitchen, where Dwight was busy cooking.

So far, Burke hadn't had a bad meal, and that just amazed him because Dwight was cooking on his own. Surely there were plenty of days where he probably wished somebody else would take over the cooking. Burke was a fine hand with a steak, but, when it came to so much of the other stuff, it just wasn't the same. Toby was a great cook himself, and Burke knew that, between Dwight and Toby, the rest of them would get along just fine. Even without those two main cooks, these guys would somehow make it just fine, even cooking for themselves. Yet it was really nice to have Dwight around, taking on the bulk of the cooking, with Big

Toby helping when he could, since a lot of guys were here to feed still.

As Burke walked inside the main log cabin, he stopped and took a look outside. "Is that the doe I've heard so much about?" he asked, pointing.

Timber peered out the window and smiled. "Yeah, that's her. … You can see her fawn, just a little bit away from her," he murmured. "It's really great seeing them here."

"It is, but how do you keep them away from Billy Bob?"

"So far, he hasn't been an issue. I don't know if a bobcat would attack a deer. I suppose, if he's hungry, he might try to get to the fawn, but he never seems to be hungry when he's here." Then Timber laughed. "Plus, Dwight's got a soft spot for Billy Bob, giving him some choice leftovers. Then again Dwight has a soft spot for every living being. Toby is another favorite."

"Yeah? Which one, the man or the dog?" Burke asked, shaking his head. "Little Toby loves to play with Big Toby, and our Toby just thinks it's a perfect pairing."

"It's a great pairing," Timber declared, with a laugh. "I told Big Toby that we should change his dog's name, but Toby seems to like the fact that he's got his own namesake. And Toby likes the dog no matter what we call him."

"I understand, but it sure makes it a little bit frustrating sometimes when we call for one, and the other shows up. I don't think I've ever gotten the one I wanted."

Timber laughed. "And that's the way of it sometimes."

As they walked into the dining area and took a seat, Burke's phone rang, and everybody looked up. He checked the screen, frowned, and shut off the ringer.

"If you want to take a call, feel free," Tommy suggested. "We're not being nosy. We're just interested in everybody else's life because we don't have one of our own."

Burke snorted. "No, it's all good. It's nobody I wanted to talk to."

"Ooh, … sounds like a divorce."

He frowned at him and asked, "Divorce? Where would you get that?"

Tommy laughed and explained, "While my wife was busy divorcing me, I used to get phone messages from her and the lawyers all the time, and I hated them. They were always fussing over some of the darndest things that I just couldn't see were worth even talking about. I mean, my world was collapsing around me, and she wanted to argue about a couch." He shook his head.

The others chipped in a variety of sympathetic comments, along with a few jokes.

Tommy continued. "Really, it just pointed out how very different we were and how much I needed to move on, but still, it wasn't my choice," he admitted. "So, … if I make jokes about it, sorry. It's just my way of dealing with it."

"It's all good," Burke replied. "Sometimes we need to joke away the pain in our lives. Yet the silly thing is, there's no divorce in my world. There's no divorce because there's no marriage."

"Ouch," Tommy muttered, "that sounds as if you were hoping there would have been one."

Burke snorted. "You guys are great at making up stuff, but honestly, no mystery is here, and no girl was on the phone. Just somebody pretty disgruntled in life, and I don't know what to tell him because I don't—"

"Have a clue?" Tommy suggested, with a mock smile.

Burke stared at Tommy for a moment, then shook his head, "It's the strangest thing. This guy's been calling and calling, and I keep telling him that I don't have a clue who he's after or who he wants me to talk to him about. He keeps asking for a guy with my name, which is already pretty strange because I've never run across another person named Burke Thomas out there. Then we have this whole conversation about how I ripped him off. I don't know who the guy is who's calling me, and I didn't rip anybody off. I've told him that repeatedly, but he insists that I'm lying and that somebody out there with my name has been ripping people off."

Tommy frowned. "He could be telling the truth. I mean, it's possible you've had your identity stolen," he suggested, staring at him. "You should probably take a look at that."

"How the hell would I even do that though?" Burke asked, staring at the man in shock. "That's hardly something I can just turn around and figure out. *Here, let's go see if somebody has taken over my identity.*"

"No, but there are people who can do that for you," Timber shared.

Big Toby nodded. "Plenty of stories are out there of people making a great living by stealing identities these days," Big Toby pointed out. "So, it would be rough if it were true, but it would explain things if this guy is irritated and is blaming you for something you know nothing about."

"What am I supposed to do though?" Burke asked, staring at him. "I haven't done shit to anyone."

"No, but, if it's done under your name, you could still be liable for it," Tommy noted, turning to look him in the eye.

"That's not fair."

"Lots of things in life aren't fair," Timber noted, raising

one eyebrow.

Tommy agreed. "Life isn't fair, and all of us gathered here today know that very well." Tommy grimaced, shook his head, then went back to talking to the other men.

Burke didn't know Tommy very well, but, since Burke had been at Timber's, it was definitely easier to get to know these guys, as he worked with them day in and day out. Yet some of them just weren't all that forthcoming about what was going on in their world, so Burke was surprised to hear this one talking as much as he was.

Tommy was fairly young, and, in a way, that was good because it also meant he might have a little more experience with the digital world that the rest of them didn't have.

Burke admitted, "I wouldn't even know where to start with this."

"I have a friend who could take a look," Tommy suggested, "but you may not like the results."

"No, I might not," Burke agreed, shaking his head, "but, if somebody really is out there doing shit under my name, I should probably find out."

"I agree," Tommy stated. "Okay, I can give him a call."

After dinner Tommy came and sat down beside Burke. "Hey, I talked to that buddy of mine, and he agreed to take a look for you."

"Awesome, so what does he need from me?"

"He'll call you and go over that," Tommy replied. "He's a digital PI who searches people's identities."

"Didn't even know there was such a thing," Burke noted, staring at him.

"He works for some big companies, making sure that things are clean on the internet for their brands and that sort of thing. So, he might be able to help you. It just seems weird that you keep getting phone calls and that this guy is so adamant. At least if you found out something concrete, proving that it wasn't you, he might leave you alone."

"That would be good," Burke murmured. "Thanks."

"Yeah, it's all good." With that, Tommy got up and moved over to sit with one of the other guys. Burke glanced over at Timber, who was staring at Tommy, then shrugged.

Timber shook his head. "It's the world we live in now, it seems," he pointed out. "I'm not as digital savvy as I want to be, and honestly, I keep off the internet a lot just because I think too much of a mess is out there already. Still, if this can help you out," he noted, "it could be huge."

"I agree, and I don't even see it as a problem, except this guy calling me is pretty adamant. The whole identity theft thing hadn't occurred to me."

"And, if your caller is adamant and is getting increasingly upset with you about all this, you should nip it in the bud as soon as you can. Just because he's accusing you of something doesn't mean it's for real, but it could mean that somebody out there is taking advantage, and you don't want that."

# CHAPTER 2

WHEN THE PHONE call came in later that night, Burke was surprised, as he'd just come out of the shower, was tired, and had stretched out on his bed. He almost didn't answer the call, but remembering what Tommy had said earlier, Burke picked up the call and wasn't surprised that it was Gregory, Tommy's friend. Burke talked with him for a few minutes and explained the situation.

Gregory went quiet for quite a while, while the sound of a keyboard clacking away filled the cell phone. Finally Gregory shared, "I'm already going through some of the stuff online about you. Have you checked your credit cards?"

"I shut them down a few weeks ago," he replied, with a yawn.

"I'm not sure about that because we've still got active credit cards showing in your name."

Burke sat up, shocked. "What? What are you talking about?" And it didn't take long for Burke to realize that credit cards in his name were being used, even using his last known address. He swore at that and asked, "How do I shut them down?"

"Not only that but you'll have to do something to stop people from getting new ones," Gregory muttered. "We'll have some work to do here. Look. I'll call you tomorrow. I know it's late right now."

"What will you do?"

"I'll send you a list of the credit cards I found so far and what companies issued them. Then I'll do some more research tonight on this. Meanwhile, you call these credit card companies first and tell them of the fraud. Thereafter, contact the three credit reporting bureaus and put a freeze on any new debt in your name. So we'll get this canned from that end. I do this professionally, and some of the groups I can deal with on my own," he muttered, "but you will have to make the calls on some of these. Anyway, I'll get back to you in the morning." And, with that, he disconnected.

The call left Burke with a bad taste in his mouth as he realized that somebody else had credit cards in his name and that this could be a way bigger problem than he could imagine. As soon as he closed his eyes, everything just piled in on top of him, and it was hard to sleep. He finally got up, walked downstairs, and headed outside to sit on the deck in the cooler night air, as he considered it all.

Big Toby joined him a little bit later. "You okay?"

"I don't know," he admitted. "I just talked to Gregory."

"Who's that?"

"Tommy's friend, the digital PI. Apparently multiple credit cards have been issued in my name that somebody else is using."

"That sucks," Toby replied, as he stared at him in shock.

"I agree. So Gregory will do an extended search tonight and will get back in touch with me in the morning and share any more findings," Burke explained, "but it does make me more than a little concerned."

Just then his phone rang again. He checked the ID on his phone screen and frowned. "Shirley is calling me?"

Big Toby pointed at Burke's cell. "I don't know who

that is, but, judging by the look on your face, you better answer it, given everything else going on in your world."

So Burke did, and it was a familiar voice, but one he hadn't heard from in a while.

"Burke, is that you?" she asked.

"Yeah, it's me. Is that really you, Shirley?"

"It is, indeed," she confirmed, with a half laugh. "I wasn't sure if you would pick up."

"Honestly, I wasn't sure either, as some weird shit's been happening."

"What do you mean by weird shit?" she asked cautiously.

"Why don't you tell me why you're calling?" When she hesitated, he asked, "Has this got something to do with my ex?"

She snorted. "Meaning my sister? ... Yes. I just happened to see something that she had. I'm not sure how she got it, or what she's doing, but ..."

Something clicked in Burke's mind. "Does she have a credit card in my name?" he asked bluntly. "Because I just found out that somebody has opened several credit card accounts in my name."

She gasped. "So, you didn't give it to her?"

He froze and then barked, "Of course I didn't give it to her. What are you talking about?"

"She told me that you gave it to her to help her out."

"No, no way," he cried out. "When did she do this?"

"Just recently, but she told me that you gave it to her. She was speaking really fast though, so I was scared she was lying."

"Of course she was lying," he snapped. "Good Christ. If she's racked up a ton of money ..."

"I'm afraid she probably has. You know what she's like."

"I do know what she's like. Remember one of the reasons we broke up?"

"I know. I know, but, when I saw the credit card, I just didn't know what to do."

"I do appreciate your letting me know that it's her because it's literally happening right now."

"Oh, crap. So you've already gotten alerts?"

"I've been getting phone calls from some angry older guy because apparently I had bought some stuff from him and the payment bounced back as invalid, but the stuff's already been picked up. It was some handmade furniture or something."

There was silence on the other end, then Shirley sighed. "Oh my God, that's Benji. Silvia told me that he made it for her."

"I'm sure he did."

"She also told me that she paid for it."

"Yeah, with my fake credit card, and the charge didn't go through or something."

"Yeah, and he knows her, so he let her take the furniture, probably after she told him that *you* would pay for it. And now she probably isn't responding to Benji's calls, and he's got your number instead."

"Yeah, you're not kidding," Burke muttered, hanging his head. "Benji calls all the time about me screwing over people and not paying for things that I bought."

"I'm so sorry," she wailed.

"What the hell, Shirley?"

"I didn't know how bad this was. Plus she's got a new boyfriend, which is how I really knew that you weren't paying for it."

"Ya think?" He sat here, stunned. "I don't even know what to say right now."

"I'm so sorry. If she finds out I told you all this, she'll really blow up."

"What does she expect you to do?" he snapped.

"Look. I don't think she knows where you are, even what state you're in." Then she asked, "Where are you anyway?" When he hesitated, she added, "No, of course, you don't want to tell me. Why would you. I'm so sorry, Burke."

"Look. I'm not against telling you where I am, but it won't help you in this scenario."

"Maybe," she conceded, "but I do need to tell you that the boyfriend is pretty ugly though."

"Pretty ugly?"

"I don't mean physically ugly," she clarified, tripping over her words.

"What are you saying?"

"I think he's dangerous," she clarified, the words rushing out of her mouth. "He's not a good influence on her at all."

"Ya think?" he repeated, with a dry laugh. "She was somebody who definitely couldn't be trusted around money and credit cards, but she didn't use to be somebody who stole identities."

"Oh my gosh," she cried out. "I didn't even think of it in that way, but that's what it is, isn't it?"

"Yeah, there's a name for it," he stated. "Credit card fraud. This is jailtime stuff." When she gasped, he added, "Silvia's not even using her head here. Did she think I wouldn't find out? Is she thinking at all?"

"No, she isn't, and, if she finds out that I told you about this card, she'll blame me."

"And is that a problem?"

"Well …"

Burke asked. "Shirley, will your sister hurt you?"

"My sister won't, but her boyfriend? I'm not so sure. His name is Jacob or something like that, but he goes by Jay. He's just, I don't know, he's kind of …"

"Okay, he's what? Just say it."

"He's dangerous, and he's scary. I don't want to be around him at all, especially when I realized what she was doing and who she was doing it to, I got really angry, and she just laughed it off. She told me that you deserved it for leaving her the way you did."

"I deserve it for leaving her? She'd racked up my credit cards more times than I could count. I had to close all those accounts and cut them all up because of her. Plus, there were a few other major things that broke us up, like she had an affair," he spat.

"I know. I know, but my sister has changed."

"I don't think Silvia has changed at all, at least not for the better," he noted. "I think she's exactly who she always was, but she just did a better job of keeping all that hidden back then."

"But she's in trouble now," Shirley muttered.

"Please don't tell me that you're calling to ask me to help your sister."

She hesitated. "I guess that would be really pushing things, wouldn't it?"

"Yeah, it definitely would, particularly right now," he declared, with a snort. "You do realize I'll have to call the cops in on this?"

After a moment of silence, she muttered, "That's probably the best thing … honestly."

"But it doesn't sound as if you're very happy about it."

"It's my sister," Shirley stated, her tone bitter. "Of course I'm not happy about it, but she's messing with your life now too."

"No, it's well beyond *messing with my life*," he stated. "I've got a PI literally doing an investigation, trying to figure out what's going on. He found the maxed-out credit card accounts in my name, and who knows what else he might find. It's not a pretty sight, Shirley. It's identity theft."

"I'm so sorry," she whispered. "Look. … I'm in New Mexico, and I have been for the last, I don't know, six months or so. I'm in between Albuquerque and Santa Fe. I don't know quite where you are, but, if I can do anything to help, just say it."

"The police will need to talk to you."

She sighed. "Jay won't like that."

"*He* won't?"

"No, … *they* won't."

"They will just have to deal with it," he snapped. "I want my name cleared, and I want these bills paid, and I, for damn sure, will not be paying them."

"They don't have any money," she exclaimed, then snorted. "Yet they do, but I don't know where they get it from."

"I do. They're probably taking cash advances off the damn credit cards," he cried out.

After a bit of silence, she added, "I have to go. You've got my number." And, with that, she disconnected, and Burke stared out into the darkness.

Big Toby muttered, "Now that is messed up."

Burke turned to face him. "Sorry, I forgot you were there."

"Hey, dude, you can keep forgetting I'm here because

that's just wrong."

"I know," he agreed. "So that was Shirley, the sister of my ex-girlfriend, and I just don't know what I'm supposed to do."

"You know exactly what to do. You call the cops, and that shit will stop. You need to get all those credit cards reported as fraudulently opened, and you need to stay on the lookout for more. That is exactly why you have to involve the police, so you'll have a police report documenting things."

"Shit, I don't want to get Shirley in trouble either."

"You may not have to, considering that you've already got this digital PI guy checking what's going on with these credit cards, plus the other guy who keeps calling you."

"Sure, Gregory's already told me that somebody out there is using my fake cards, and now I know who it is—*Silvia*."

"Right." Toby nodded. "The local police department in town can take the report and can arrange to have anybody picked up who needs to be picked up, even in another state."

"They're probably in New Mexico," Burke muttered. "That's where they were before, and that's apparently where Shirley is."

"Don't let them come over here," Big Toby stated. "None of us need anything to do with people like that."

"I agree," Burke confirmed. "I came here to get away from Silvia and to forget it all. It got pretty ugly there at the end, but it's been quite a while."

"And what about Shirley, the sister?"

"Shirley is great," he said, with a sad smile. "Honestly, out of the entire family, she's the only one who's decent. Even their father is a con artist."

"Yeah, but there's a difference between a con artist and a complete fraud," Big Toby pointed out. "Seems Silvia's gotten herself into something pretty major now."

"I agree, and yet I suspect she will try to spin it as being a bit of a joke, something she could get out of because she's always been given a free pass," Burke muttered.

Big Toby asked, "Who gave her a free pass?"

"Almost everyone in her life. Even me. When it came down to it, I just didn't want to cause any fuss," he explained, "so I just let it go, paid the bills, and got out of there."

"That's why she keeps getting away with this shit."

"I know. I know, and that's just wrong," he muttered.

"Get some sleep. I suggest that, first thing in the morning, you file a report with the local authorities, contact the credit card companies, tell them it's fraud, and dispute the cards and the charges made."

"Gregory told me that he was already contacting them, but that I would need to contact them too. I don't even have the details of how many cards are out there and what companies the cards are with, not to mention how much she's run up." Burke groaned. "I don't know everything that's been done, but Gregory will send me a full report in the morning."

"Good. You jump on all that. You for sure don't want Silvia to have any advance notice that you are on to her."

"Shirley also mentioned that Silvia's boyfriend is dangerous," he shared. "If they go after Shirley, she doesn't have anybody in her corner. Her father has always been against her because she wouldn't go down the same criminal pathway that he and Silvia chose."

"Who else is in the family?" Toby asked.

"Just the father and the two daughters. The dad is all in, and, if a con works, you take it for all you can, then you run. The last thing I want is for them to run right now."

"The last thing you want is for them to continuously blow up your credit too, just because they can. I hate to bring this up, but who knows if it's just limited to credit cards?"

"Shit," Burke muttered.

"And, if this boyfriend is dangerous, what else has he done?"

"I don't know, but you can bet I don't really want to take a closer look."

"You may not have a choice," Toby noted.

"The bottom line is, I don't want anything to happen to Shirley for having told me."

"I get that," Toby murmured, "but you also have to take care of yourself." And, with that, Toby got up and left.

# CHAPTER 3

S HIRLEY STARED DOWN at her phone, not quite
believing that she had gotten up the nerve to let Burke
know what was happening. She feared she wouldn't get
much sleep tonight.

She woke up the next morning and stared around at the
small apartment she'd rented. She'd been doing odd jobs for
the last year, just trying to figure out what she wanted to do
with the rest of her life. She had project management
experience, and she'd held that position at a big company,
but the stress had been crippling to the point that she had
quit.

Her mental health needed rather desperately to find a
new career path. It had been great until it wasn't, and she
needed to take a break from all that stress. Right now, she
was working as a receptionist, while she figured out her life.
She desperately wanted to get away from her family, yet the
guilt crippled her. They were family, and she loved them,
but she didn't like them at all, and that was really hard on
her.

The following morning her sister called, a happy-go-
lucky tone in her voice. "Hey, Shir, we're going out for
breakfast. Want to come with? My treat."

"What? On Burke's credit cards?" she snapped.

Silvia laughed. "Yeah, … on his credit card. Why the

hell not?"

"How can you do that?"

"Oh please, don't you start with that pious bullshit," her sister snapped. "He fucking broke up with me. He deserves everything he gets."

"He broke up with you because the relationship wasn't working. You were sleeping with another man."

"Yeah, it wasn't working, and it's not working now either," she barked. "Besides, he won't know."

"Yeah, but are you paying the bills?"

"No, ... of course not." She laughed. "The credit cards will get canceled eventually, and we'll just ... carry on."

"So, you've done this before?" she asked in horror.

"No, I haven't, but Frankie has. He learned from his poppa Jensen."

Shirley took note of the name, as she had mentioned to Burke that his name was Jay, short for Jacob, and she needed to update him.

"He says that's how he always does it, that it's a great system," she explained. "So, we live a decent life, and we don't have to pay the bills."

"So, you're screwing somebody over every time you do this, and you don't care?"

"Of course I don't care, and why should I? I tried hard to be a nice person and look what happened."

"Yeah? What happened?" she asked angrily. "Nothing. You've never tried."

"What are you talking about? He broke up with me."

Shirley groaned. "Silvia, you know perfectly well that you weren't happy with him, and you were out screwing around on him."

"So what?" she replied vindictively. "He's still not allowed to break up with me."

"That's crap," she muttered. "You always look at everything in a backassward way," she muttered.

"And you always blame me."

"No, I'm not blaming you. I just don't understand how you have absolutely no morals and expect the entire world to look after you, when you do nothing responsibly to look after yourself."

"I do a lot to look after myself," she cried out. "And that's exactly what I'm doing. I'm looking after me instead of having somebody else come in and steal everything and have the life that I should have had."

Shirley argued, "He wasn't responsible for your not having the life that you should have had."

"Look. If you care about him so much, you should have gone after him."

"I should have. … You're right," Shirley snapped, "because I did care about him, but you screwed all that over too."

"Oh, … what the hell, Shir?" Silvia snapped right back. "He won't know anything about it—at least not until he tries to buy a house and his credit is completely destroyed or when the bill collectors come after him. He's probably got a new car or something," she said vindictively. "I wish I could see the look on his face when he realizes that it's been repossessed to pay for the credit cards."

Shirley stared down at her phone, listening to her sister in complete shock. "I don't even know you anymore."

"There's nothing to know." Silvia cackled with joy. "I've always been this way. You just didn't want to see it."

That was similar to what Burke had said too, but it was even harder to hear it coming out of her sister's own mouth.

"I didn't think you hated people quite so much."

"I don't hate him," she stated. "I'm pissed off at what he did, but I don't hate him."

"How can you be pissed off at what he did? He didn't do anything but get himself out of a mess."

"Of course he did something," she spat.

"Right, he broke up with you."

"Look. It might not be a big deal to you, but it hurt me."

"You'd already had an affair, and I don't know how many times you'd run up bills in his name."

"I don't care," Silvia bellowed. "He was supposed to try harder. That's what you do. You try harder. You hold on to the people you claim you love."

"Did *you* try harder?" she asked her sister.

"That wasn't for me to do. That was for him to do. Why can't you understand that? No wonder you don't have a partner. God, how did you miss all those lessons?"

"Maybe because I was busy trying to be a good person."

She snorted at that. "Yeah, and where did it get you? *Nowhere.*" Silvia added, "Don't bother coming to breakfast. You've ruined the mood." And, with that, she ended the call.

"Oh, jeez, as if I was going anyway. Unlike you, I wouldn't expect Burke to pay for my breakfast," she muttered out loud, then groaned.

She sent Burke a quick text. **Hate to say it, but she's headed out for breakfast on your credit cards again.** She got a response right back.

**Shouldn't go through now because those credit cards have been canceled.**

Shirley winced and sent back a text. **All three of them?**

He phoned her immediately. "Did you say she has three

credit cards in my name?"

"Yes," and she named off the companies.

"Wow, so more phone calls," he muttered.

"I'm so sorry."

"Stop saying that. I know you're sorry, but I highly doubt you could have stopped her."

"Actually she called me all kinds of names because I wasn't interested in going out and having breakfast … on you."

"She what?"

"Yeah, she called to invite me out to breakfast, *her treat*, and I mentioned something about it being on your credit card, and she went off on what a brilliant way it was to live."

"Jesus," he muttered.

She heard the fury starting to build in Burke's tone. "I'm sorry."

He froze. "Shirley, stop—"

"I know. I know. I need to stop saying that."

"You really struggle with that, don't you?"

"A lifetime of guilt will do that," she muttered.

"Yeah, your family is a bit of a mess in that way, aren't they?"

"*A bit*," she repeated, with a broken laugh. "Who am I kidding? You know them all too well. Both of them are a mess."

"How is your dad?"

"Running a new con, according to Silvia. I don't know what it is and don't want to know."

"I hope it's got nothing to do with me." Burke gave a heavy sigh. "I gather the new boyfriend gets along really well with him."

"Yeah, this guy has a history of racking up credit cards

until the cards get canceled. Then they move on to some-body else. And I forgot to tell you, today she called him Frankie."

"Frankie. ... *Great*."

"She's hoping you find out about it the hard way, when your vehicle gets repossessed to pay these bills or when you go buy a house and have shit for credit."

"Jesus, I forgot how nice of a person she is," he quipped.

Still, Shirley heard the anger in his tone. "I know. I'm—" Then she froze.

"Yeah, I know. You're sorry." He sighed. "Listen. I need to get to work. Thanks for the update." With that, he disconnected.

She didn't even know what to say. What could she say?

Her family was a complete mess, and, in her own way, Shirley had done nothing but enable them because she didn't know what else to do. How do you turn in your own family and not have them turn on you like rabid animals? She tried to shut off even thinking about her family as she arrived at work, sitting at the receptionist's desk, answering the phone calls and greeting the people walking in.

Very quickly though, she got a phone call. A personal phone call at work. She was busy with the incoming lines when it came through for her. When she explained that she was at work, she realized it was the police. "Oh, crap."

"I understand that you know something about a credit card scenario involving Burke Thomas."

"Yes, I do," she confirmed.

"I need you to come in and talk to me."

"I will, but I can't do it right now."

"May I ask why?"

"I'm at work, and I really need my job."

"I can certainly understand that."

The telephone discussion continued, and they made arrangements for the afternoon when she got off work. But, for the rest of the day, all she could do was turn around, looking at every door, to see who would be coming in, afraid that Silvia might somehow have found out that Shirley worked here. She also realized that, as soon as her sister *did* find out where Shirley was working, she would be in trouble and should be prepared to make a quick move and find yet another job. Just the thought was enough to make her sick.

By the time she got through work today, she was a nervous wreck. She walked to the police station to talk to the man who had called her. As she stepped inside and spoke to the front desk, she was directed to a small table. When she sat down, the man came over and joined her.

"I'm Detective Martin. Thanks for coming in. Do you want to explain what's going on?"

She winced. "I can, but …"

"But what?"

"My sister's boyfriend is dangerous," she shared. "I know this is my sister's fault, and I know that this is the right thing to do, but I really don't want them to find out that I told you about them."

He stared at her steadily for a long moment. "How dangerous?"

She winced. "I'm pretty sure that a good solid beating would be the least of my worries."

He frowned at that and nodded. "You want to start with their names?"

Reluctantly she gave him her sister's name and what she knew about the boyfriend. "I don't know if that's his real name. That's just the name I know him as. She called him

Jay one time, but recently, as of this morning, she called him Frankie, so now I'm not sure at all."

At the name, the detective clicked on his computer and shared, "I have another man here in the system." Then he gave her the name. At that, she winced. "That's my father." He turned to face her, and she nodded. "He's done time for fraud, and my sister has now picked up a boyfriend who appears to be taking her along the same pathway."

"And yet she did this on her own."

"I don't know if she would have done it without his influence, but, either way, she's definitely capable at this point, and happily so," she grumbled, with a nod.

"Are you in communication with your father?"

She snorted. "No. I'm not by any means a beloved child."

"And why is that?"

"Because I've chosen a different path for my life."

"What do you mean?"

She shrugged. "My father doesn't see any point in working and thinks it's much better to steal or to defraud somebody of their money because he didn't have to do the work for it."

"So, he doesn't think there's any work involved in defrauding people?" he asked. "Because most of the criminals who we nabbed have put a fair bit of work into it."

"If it's work, maybe he doesn't see it as work when it's a con," she suggested, frowning. "Meaning that I think it's more of a game to him."

"Now that makes more sense, … yes. Do they know how you feel about it?"

"Oh yes," she declared, "and that's the problem. I have been very vocal about my lack of interest in their lifestyle for a very long time, but they really don't care, and they are who they are. They think I'm some stupid chump for having jobs and earning my own way."

"So, why are you involved in this case now?"

"Because it involves someone I know and consider as a friend," she shared. "The guy who Silvia's defrauding, Burke Thomas, is her ex-boyfriend. She somehow managed to open up three credit card accounts in his name and has been living it up on them, and he knew nothing about it. He's a war veteran," she explained, "and, while they were together, she continually charged up his credit cards. He finally had enough of it and cut up and canceled those cards before she could do more damage. She says that basically he owes her this."

"Oh, does he now?" Detective Martin snorted. "Of course, it doesn't matter to her that he was out there serving the country while she was sitting at home doing nothing, right?"

"Exactly, and my family doesn't have any respect for veterans. Burke was injured pretty badly, and I think maybe she thought it would be a really nice affluent life for her, and she could sit back and be queen of the day, without having to do anything."

The detective lifted his head from his notebook and stared at her. "So, depending on how long he served and the extent of his injuries, there's likely a pension, but that doesn't mean big money."

"No, of course not. So here he was, trying to find work, plus he was recovering from multiple surgeries, and Silvia was grossed out about that," she admitted. "She was clearly in it for the money."

"But there was no money?" he asked.

"Apparently not what she was expecting." When he nodded, she went on. "Then, when he finally had enough and broke up with her, she took it personally."

"Why did he break up with her?"

"She was spending his money without his permission, and she also had an affair," she pointed out and watched as his eyebrows shot up. "I didn't say that she was particularly smart, but she is extremely beautiful and very manipulative. On the surface, she's extremely easy to talk to and friendly," she added, then fell silent.

"In other words, when he came back and was a bit of an easy mark, particularly if he was disabled or injured in any way, she just stepped right in and took advantage."

"Yeah, something like that," she muttered. "And, no, I have no love for my sister over it all. In fact, I don't even recognize her anymore. Maybe I've just had blinders on, but it's got to stop. Obviously the choices my father and my sister have made have distanced me from my family, and this is more of the same. However, now Silvia has this boyfriend, and he, … he really scares me," she whispered. "Frankie and I think the last name is Jenson."

The detective's gaze narrowed, as he added, "He's not coming up in the database as having any record."

"And I don't know if he does or not, but Silvia told me that he's done this many times." she shared. "All I know is, when I do see them, there's always that look in his eyes."

"What look?"

"That look that says, *I better be doing what I'm supposed to be doing—or else.*"

"And what are you supposed to be doing?"

"Presumably keeping my mouth shut."

"So, you're here at a certain amount of risk."

"Yes," she declared. "As much as I hate to even think of it, I suspect that my sister will be at risk whenever she ceases to be useful too."

He nodded at that. "That's not very different from any other con that's being run. They have a group of people they work with, and, when you have lost your usefulness, you become a liability," he explained, "and it seems Silvia might be up against that soon."

"That is my worry," Shirley muttered. "I've been hoping that something would go wrong between them, and she would break up with him, but she's not showing any signs of that."

He just nodded and kept taking notes.

Shirley asked, "Is there anything you can do to help Burke?"

"We've got calls in to him, and he's coming into town to talk to us." He looked at his watch and noted, "He should be here pretty soon."

"Burke's coming here?" she asked, struggling to keep the delight out of her tone.

"Yeah." Just then, his phone buzzed. "If I'm lucky, that would be him right now. Give me a minute." He stood up and left the area.

She sat back and looked around, wondering if she would be lucky enough for it to be him. And, sure enough, when she turned to look up again, he stood there, smiling at her. She hopped up, and, when he opened his arms, she gave him a great big hug. "Oh, my goodness," she muttered. "You're looking fabulous and all healed up."

"I've been, well, … I was doing a whole lot better until I heard what your sister was up to."

"I know. I'm …"

Immediately he placed a finger across her lips. "I know you're sorry. This has just been a shit show from the beginning."

"I know. I know," she agreed, "and I'm really hoping they can do something for you."

"Me too, but I'm worried about this Frankie guy … and you."

"Me too," she murmured. "I was hoping," she began, with half a laugh, "that maybe he was wanted or something, and they would just pick him up, and he would be out of our lives, but it doesn't seem I'll be quite so lucky."

"And that's not necessarily an easy answer either," Burke noted, "because jail isn't forever."

"Right, I hadn't thought of that."

Just then Detective Martin came back over and sat down. "Now, let's go over the details."

"What more do you need from me?" Shirley asked.

"I'll just need you to sign your statements, and then you can go."

She smiled and nodded, and, with that, they got down to business.

# CHAPTER 4

S TANDING OUTSIDE THE police station, Burke turned to
Shirley. "Time for coffee?"

She nodded. "Sure," she replied, with a bright smile. "I
really am happy to see you. It was such a shock to hear what
my sister was up to."

"I remember being shocked a couple times, hearing some
of the things that came out of her mouth," he shared, "but I
apparently never really understood just how depraved she
had gotten. It just seemed as if she were ..." He frowned as
he thought about it. "I don't even know how to describe it,
but it was almost like she just didn't really realize that my
money wasn't a freefall for her."

"That's pretty accurate. I don't know where she got that
from either because it's not as if we had a lot of money
growing up. But you know, my dad always had credit cards,"
she noted, with a frown. "Credit cards and cash, and,
looking back, I don't even know where he got half of that
from, especially since he wasn't the type to work. And yet he
would say that I owe him for having raised me."

"Of course he would. I'm not sure that's an accurate
term, since it's not as if he raised you. It's more about you
had no choice in the matter as to who your birth father was."

"Sure, but he would still say that he put the food on the
table and that I owe him for that," she added.

"You could always go *no contact*."

"I pretty well am with my father. I haven't spoken to him in a very long time. A year or two, maybe even three, now that I think about it." She shook her head. "Silvia is in touch with him all the time, probably mostly because the boyfriend gets along with him. Two peas in a pod." When she slid her glance sideways at him, he shook his head.

"And, no, … I'm not missing her or carrying a torch for her," he declared. "It was over pretty fast, once I realized who she really was, even though I didn't know the half of it."

"Yeah, sometimes I think she should come with a warning label."

He laughed at that. "She absolutely should, and how sad is that?"

"Which is true, so why do I feel as if I'm being disloyal."

"No," he stated, facing her. "If and when you had family members who cared about people—instead of sizing them up as a potential mark, then ripping them off—you would be all for them," he suggested.

She frowned but listened quietly.

"As a child, you're not responsible for your parents or anything about them," he stated. "But when you become an adult, you become responsible for how much you have to do with them. And, if they're involved in illegal activities, you've got to set boundaries. Otherwise you'll just get sucked into that madness with them."

"Which I've always worked very hard to avoid."

"Yes, but now it's crunch time, isn't it? Because now you know how much damage they are causing to so many other people that the onus is on you to do something about it."

"Which I am," she pointed out, "and the cost to me could be hefty."

"Yes, and I am definitely appreciative of that fact."

"I really wish she didn't have this boyfriend," she muttered.

"You *really* think he's dangerous?"

"I know he's dangerous," she declared, with a shudder. "He has this look in his eyes when he stares at me."

"If he shows any interest in you, your sister won't handle that well."

"Neither will I," she muttered. "He is so not anybody I want around me. I mean, … you've been gone a year," she said, with a frown.

"Something like that, … maybe ten months."

"And she hooked up with him right away."

"He might be the one she was involved with while I was still with her," he noted, "and, if that's the case, she's been with him quite a while then."

"And that could be. She didn't tell me about him very early on, and even then I knew she was going out with somebody new, but she didn't tell me the details. It's better that way," she conceded. "I don't really want to know the details of her life. I don't want to know anything about her. I really just want to live a life without them. They're not very far from here, but I've been trying to figure out what I wanted to do with my life now."

"I thought you had some project management gig," he replied. "Are you not still doing that?"

"No, the stress was killing me."

He frowned as he thought about that. "I do remember you coming home after work, visiting with us or something, and you were absolutely racked."

"Yeah, that's about the size of it," she muttered. "The project management field is incredibly hard, and, with everything else going on, I just didn't need the extra stress. Yet it's also where my training is, but I'm currently working as a receptionist. My sister finds that hilarious because I trained hard and went through all that, whereas she did absolutely nothing, and she's living better than I am." His jaw worked, and she nodded. "Of course she's living better because she's not working, because she's living on everybody else," she noted. "I get that, but it's still a slam in the face."

"Of course it is," he agreed, "and nobody likes that, particularly when you know that she's cheating to get that edge over you."

"And yet she's not doing it to get the edge over me. That's just an extra perk. She's doing it because she feels perfectly entitled," she explained.

"That's the part that blows me away," he admitted, with a snort. "How is it that anybody feels so entitled that they can hurt others just to get something for themselves?"

"I don't even think that she feels so much entitled as she just doesn't care. It's providing her with the lifestyle that she wants, that she likes, and nobody is really there to stop her."

"Well, … this will stop now," he vowed. "I don't know exactly how ugly it'll get, but …"

Just then her phone rang, and it was Silvia. She placed her finger against her lips, so he wouldn't speak while she was talking to her sister.

He reached over and hit the Speaker button.

"Hey. What's up?" Shirley asked.

"What do you mean, what's up?" Silvia snapped in a snarly tone. "The credit cards got canceled," she grumbled, practically growling, "which means we couldn't pay for brunch."

"What did you expect?" she asked, with a sigh. "Obviously, at some point in time, he'll find out."

"Sure, at some point in time, but he shouldn't have found out so soon."

"What do you mean? As soon as people start checking in on their credit cards or if somebody notices a bill hasn't been paid, he was bound to figure it out."

"Yeah, but we haven't had this one so long that a bill would even be sent out, not that it would go to his address anyway, and that's the trick," she snapped. "You have to use it as heavily as you can in those first few billing cycles because, once the bills go unpaid, these companies start reaching out, sending letters and making phone calls. There are some early grace periods, but, once they start figuring out that nobody is paying, it's not long before problems set in."

"So, what you're saying is that he must have found out sooner than you expected, and now you're pissed?"

"Of course I'm pissed. I had to pay for breakfast."

Shirley's eyebrows shot up at that. "I would say I'm sorry, but, honest to God, I don't know how you expect anything different. You should have paid because you were the ones who ate it."

"It's still not fair," she grumbled.

Burke's eyebrows shoot up.

"He was always on top of his finances like that," Shirley pointed out. "You complained to me many times that you could barely buy anything without him knowing. So clearly he's used to keeping track of his credit cards."

"Sure, that's why he was always pissed at me for spending money, but he shouldn't even have known about these."

"It's not as if he gave you his credit cards to use back then in the first place, so why wouldn't he be pissed?" Shirley asked. It was a conversation she'd had with her sister many times, "And you've gone well beyond using your former boyfriend's credit cards with this deal. Opening accounts in someone else's name is beyond the pale, even for you. This is no innocent lark, Silvia, and you are just as complicit as Frankie is."

"Frankie says it got closed really fast, but that it's happened a couple times before, so it's okay. We'll just go get new ones."

"New credit cards in his name or in somebody else's name?"

"I don't know," she replied, her tone turning cagey. "I'll leave that up to Frankie."

"*Right*," she muttered. "Has Frankie ever worked?"

There was a moment of silence before Silvia replied, now anger blooming in her tone. "Don't you dare start slamming Frankie now. He's figured this shit out and that makes him smarter than anybody I know. Even Papa is a loser when it comes to Frankie."

"Did you tell Papa that?"

"No, of course not," she spat. "He's useful when we want him."

"*Right*, everybody is useful when you want them." Shirley sighed.

"You're not very useful at all. Look at you. You don't even make enough money in your job to pay your rent."

"I'm paying my rent just fine," she snapped.

"Yeah, but that's all. If you'd come to breakfast, we would have had you pay for us," she shared, and then she started to laugh. "And that's kind of like justice."

"What do you mean by justice?" she cried out.

"If it had worked out, it would have been him paying for you, and he wouldn't even have known it. But, as it turned out, it was him stiffing you, and you having to pay."

Shirley shook her head. "Whatever. Look. I'm really tired, so I'll go."

"Of course, you're tired. It's that work shit, and nobody likes it. That's why none of us do it."

Shirley scrubbed her face with her free hand. "You may not do it, but most people don't have a choice."

"But you do. You could do something completely different and a whole lot easier if you wanted to, but you don't. For whatever reason you're bound and determined to be this bloody icon of goodness," Silvia said, with a sneer.

"Okay, this is turning nasty, so, on that note, I'm getting off the phone. Good night." And when she ended the call, she then faced Burke. "Sorry you had to hear that," she muttered.

"No, it's a good thing," he clarified. "It shows me just how low she has gone and how much she doesn't care about anybody."

"No, she really doesn't," Shirley agreed. "And it's hard, it's sad, and it's making me angry and all kinds of other things that I can't describe, but there's really nothing I can do about it."

"No, she's past the point of anybody doing anything about it. She trusts this Frankie, and she doesn't seem to have the morals to live a normal life." Burke stared at her phone and shook his head. "I can't believe I even went out with her to begin with."

"The detective had an interesting take on that."

He looked over at her in surprise.

She shrugged. "Maybe I gave him the wrong impression, I don't know, but I'd mentioned that you were a veteran, recovering from multiple surgeries, and that my sister had thought you would get a very large pension, so she could live free and clear."

He just stared at her, and then he started to laugh. "If that were the case, we wouldn't have homeless vets all over the place, and so many living in single-room boarding houses, trying to survive and figuring out why they don't fit in the world anymore." He stared at her with wry humor mixed with frustration. "It's a constant problem because these men sacrificed so much and end up with so little afterward." Burke continued. "So, what are we supposed to do, when we meet up with somebody like her, and all she wants to do is destroy us more?"

Shirley didn't say anything to that.

He finally shrugged and added, "Look. It's not your problem. Sorry."

"No, it's not my problem, but I definitely feel a sense of responsibility because she's my sister."

"But you aren't responsible," he said, "and you've done the right thing now. Is this what they've been doing for money all this time? It makes me wonder how many other people they've done this to."

"I've wondered what they were living on and assumed it was something shady since there was no evidence of anyone working, but I didn't know what. When I realized that she had intentionally targeted you, I just couldn't stand by and let her do that. And, hearing her now, this is clearly at least one of the scams they are living off of, but there is no telling what else Frankie will teach her."

"I appreciate your letting me know," Burke said, as he motioned down the street. "My investigator would have figured it out, but you've helped me get a jump on it. Come on. Let's go see about that coffee."

"I want to see what they have for food. I haven't eaten yet." When he frowned at her, she shrugged. "I just got off work, and I had to come down to the police station. I didn't want to see the detective during my work hours or do anything to cause any waves with my job because I'm doing okay, but it's not as if I'm making a whole lot of money. I did make a bunch before, and I have saved some, but I don't dare let Silvia know about that."

"Does she know anything about your bank accounts?"

She frowned at that. "I would like to say no, but I can't be sure."

"Then I would highly suggest that you close your accounts, move your money, and don't let her know anything about it. If she has the slightest inkling that you have money, the day will come when she doesn't, and she'll come looking to take yours. What about your credit cards?"

She winced and shook her head. "She probably does know about those." He looked at her steadily, and she nodded slowly. "You're right. I need to protect myself, don't I?"

"Particularly if they find out you had anything to do with turning them in."

She took a couple steps, but the shock was clearly hitting her now.

He asked, "Is it a local bank?"

"Yeah, it's just around the corner." She froze, staring at him. "Good God."

"I know," he replied. "Let's not have her wipe out your money just because she can."

"Do you think she can?"

"I don't know," Burke admitted. "It depends on how you've got it locked up, who has access, and whether she's your next of kin."

"She is, and, yeah, if I die, she gets everything." Then she stopped and winced. "Jesus, please tell me that we're not having this conversation."

"You tell me. How dangerous is this boyfriend?" She just stared at him unable to stop the fear whitening, tighting her face. Burke nodded. "Come on. Let's get coffee, then we'll make a game plan."

He led her down the street to a small diner, and, as soon as they were seated, he ordered coffee and asked for menus. When the coffee came, she just sat here, staring at him, lost in her own world. He took a quick look at her, then ordered burgers for the both of them.

She protested, "No, I'm fine."

"No, you're not fine," he declared, staring at her. "Let's get you some food, and then we need to make a plan."

She stared at him. "It's just the thought that my sister would do that to me."

"So, let me take her out of the equation. Would this boyfriend do it?"

"Absolutely," she declared instantly. Then she looked at him and nodded slowly. "And that means she would probably do it too."

He just nodded and didn't say anything.

She felt the tightness in her chest as she realized how much she would have to do in order to stay safe.

"Your paychecks, does she know which accounts they go in?"

Shirley winced. "I just got paid. I can go to the bank tomorrow."

"That would be a good idea. Also, you should change your beneficiary on any of your paperwork."

She sighed and shook her head. "I don't want to think like that."

"Maybe not, but you're telling me this Frankie guy is dangerous, and, if they are short on money, that just makes them desperate enough to take money from you. I'm sure Frankie's already thought about it multiple times, as far as being a possible game."

# CHAPTER 5

SHIRLEY DIDN'T KNOW what to say to that. When the burger arrived in front of her, she started eating without even realizing it. When she was halfway through it, she stared down at her plate and frowned.

Burke laughed. "Eat," he prodded her.

"I didn't even order this," she muttered.

"No, I ordered it for you."

She groaned. "That's not fair either," she muttered, looking away. "It's not as if my sister hasn't had more than a few meals on you already."

"You're not your sister," he declared, patting her hand. "Besides, I'm hoping I can get that back."

She looked at him hopefully. "You think you can?"

"I don't know," he admitted, "but we'll give it a good try. I'm also in contact with a lawyer, one who I know works with a lot of veterans and who does a lot of *pro bono* work. A friend of mine contacted him and explained what was going on."

"That's good." She looked at him in delight. "Any help at all would be great."

"I'll take any help I can get," he added, "so don't you worry about that. It's one thing to be stubborn. It's another to be stupid."

She laughed at that and agreed. "So, what have you been

up to? You always wanted to work with animals. Are you doing anything along those lines right now?"

He grinned. "Right now I'm working *pro bono* myself, helping a friend of mine. I was looking for a place to hole up and to get my head straightened out and to figure out what I wanted to do. He's in the midst of putting together an animal sanctuary," he explained, with a smile. "I asked him if I could bunk in for a bit, and he opened his door. That's what friends are for. And, because he's in the middle of building it, I'm right in the middle of that, which works out."

"You were handy too," she muttered. "I always admired that and wished I was able to do simple stuff, but it wasn't anything I had any training or time for."

"I think that's the kind of thing you have to make time for. Either you really want to get involved in it or not. If not, really no point in worrying about it. It's one thing to have the skills from a maintenance point of view, but it's another thing entirely to have the skills as a hobby. It can be an expensive hobby, just gathering the right tools. Yet, if you enjoy it, hobbies cost money sometimes, and maybe it's worth it."

She smiled. "Either way, I'm absolutely delighted that you are invested in something. What kind of animals does he have?"

"Not too many yet because he's still building. A load of horses are coming, but I guess the vet, his girlfriend by the way, got held up, and she had to give the clearance for them to make the trip, so they're coming tomorrow. They were supposed to be here today, I think." He frowned. "Maybe it was yesterday. It seems as if I'm already losing track of time."

"And that's because you're enjoying yourself."

"I really am," he stated, with a smile. "I get that it won't be a long-term solution, and it won't pay the bills, but right now I'm helping a friend and a fellow vet who was more than willing to give me a place when I needed some respite."

"When you needed a haven," she pointed out.

He stopped, smiled, and nodded. "Exactly. And that's precisely what it's for."

"Oh, it's not just for animals?"

"He says it's for two-legged and four-legged alike." He laughed, then his expression changed. "Honestly, an awful lot of us came out of the military and didn't have a great return home. Either we have injuries or lost the people we were close to. In some cases, divorces happened very quickly, or you come home to find out that you don't have the support that you need. Just all kinds of scenarios," he muttered, with a dismissive wave. "And, for a lot of people, that becomes very difficult. My buddy had injuries to recover from himself, so he gets it. Plus, he's the kind of person who would open his doors and help, and that's essentially what he is doing."

"You have to admire that," she noted. "It sounds as if you have a real friend there."

"I do," he agreed, with a nod. "And gradually we're getting a crazy collection of animals, maybe six dogs right now and a couple cats. A squirrel lives there that he calls Dodger, plus a bobcat called Billy Bob. Danny is the donkey, and a doe with a fawn sticks pretty close to the yard."

"A doe?" she asked, looking at him.

He nodded. "Yes, a doe and her fawn. When he first saw her, she had an arrow in her shoulder. He worked to help her, and, as soon as he got the arrow out and got her stitched up and doing better, she dropped the fawn."

"Oh, how adorable," she cried out, then shook her head. "It sounds almost too good to be true."

"It is, in a way," he agreed. "A lot of work goes into it, and that's one of the reasons why we're all pitching in to help."

"Of course," she said warmly, "and, at the same time, it's helping you."

He smiled at her. "Exactly. He talks about a few other animals, but I haven't necessarily seen all of them yet. … I've been there several weeks, and we've been working nonstop." He laughed. "Honestly, I think I've worked harder physically there than I ever did in rehab."

"Maybe that's why you're doing so much better now," she suggested. "You know, with all those endorphins being released, plus the sense of satisfaction of a job well-done. I can't imagine there would be anything bad about that scenario for you."

"I don't think there's anything bad either," he agreed, staring at her. "It's always amazing when you go to help someone, and you find out just how much it's helping you."

She nodded. "Now if only I could find a solution to my situation," she muttered.

He looked over at her and nodded. "That would be good because you're in a tight spot right now."

"I know." She sighed. "I have all these uncertainties and fears about the different ways it could go, but I just don't know what I'm supposed to do."

"You did the tough part," he stated firmly, "and now it's a matter of making sure you stay safe."

"And how does one do that?" she asked. "If they even saw me with you right now, they would be shocked."

"Maybe and maybe not. Silvia used to bug me about you

all the time, suggesting that maybe I should date you instead, since I always seemed to treat you better than her." When Shirley frowned at him, he laughed. "Yeah, she used to throw that in my face all the time."

"She mentioned something similar to me just yesterday," she muttered. "I just don't know where she's coming from anymore."

"She's coming from her own space, and that's the problem," he declared, with a shrug. "It's a space that nobody else can really understand, and nobody else really wants to access. She's doing something that's important to her for whatever reason, but it'll have repercussions that I don't think she's really aware of or prepared for."

"She'll go to jail over this, won't she?"

He nodded. "I would imagine so, and, don't take this the wrong way, but I sure don't want to let her off the hook."

She winced, and her shoulders sagged as she considered that. "It's probably the best thing for her, but wow."

"I know, and going *no contact* with your family—"

"I've pretty well been there with my dad for a long time anyway," she reminded him.

"Yeah, but a couple years isn't really *no contact*," he stated. "If it was ten years, maybe."

"All of this didn't blow up ten years ago," she pointed out. "It really went ugly when the two of you broke up."

"Got it," he said, with a nod.

By the time they finished their meal, had coffee, and he ordered a piece of pie to split, she smiled. "It's hard to even imagine that we're in this scenario." He stopped to stare at her, and she winced. "Right. I get it. That was a stupid comment."

"No, ... not at all," he replied. "Anyway, I need to confirm that, when you go home, you're safe."

"They don't come around this part of town," she said, "so that's a good thing. Yet, if she has any idea that I'm involved in turning her in, it'll get ugly. And I don't think she knows you're here either. If she saw us together, ... it would make everything worse."

"Of course, and, if you need anything from me, you let me know."

"Yeah," she muttered, "but it's not as if you'll be on hand. You'll be out wherever this place is."

"That's true," he agreed, with a nod. "I'm living there right now and don't even have a home of my own at the moment. Although it's something that I think about, I don't really have a location figured out," he shared. "My buddy and I have been friends for a long time, and we served together in the military for a lot of years, so a part of me wants to stay close."

"You want to be there for him. I get it."

"When you don't have any family anymore," he shared, "staying close to what you do know and what you do have seems to be important."

"And you said he's got injuries as well?"

"Yeah, and he has somebody who has been working on prosthetics with him, who is crazy talented," he shared. "So, I'm not against having him try to get me in to see her."

"Her?" she asked.

"Yeah, she's pretty well-known for the work she does."

"Interesting."

"She's missing a leg too, and her husband has a couple prosthetics as well. So, I guess it's a natural progression of being unhappy with what was available to her all the years she was growing up."

"Interesting." Shirley frowned. "I think about these people who are doing such fabulous things, and I always feel as if I should have done so much more. I could have done so much more, and there's always that feeling of it's being too late."

He shook his head. "That's just not true. It's never too late. If you want to go back to school or something, go back to school."

She shook her head. "Not sure I'm up for that," she admitted. "There's something about school when you're younger versus school when you're older. It just doesn't have that same feel to it."

"Maybe not, but, if you're unhappy with the life that you are living, then you should do something about it."

She smiled and nodded. "I hear you, and I appreciate the advice."

He laughed. "But you don't need to listen to it, is that it?"

"No, I didn't mean that," she protested. "It's just, … until I decide what to do, it doesn't matter what the suggestions are. I still have to figure it out and commit to something."

He tilted his head and noted, "That's a very valid point. And, because of that, I will stay quiet and will let you do you."

She smiled. "It's the same thing you're doing," she pointed out.

"It is, and that's one of the reasons why I'm happy to let you do it," he admitted, and then he hesitated. "But I'm not against staying in touch if you want to," he offered, an odd look in his gaze.

She stared at him. "Are you serious? You still want that, after what my family has done to you?"

"That's your family, not you," he pointed out.

She frowned at that. "I wonder if I would be so generous."

"I would hope so," he said. "But I don't think it's easy on anybody when you have people pulling the crap that your sister and her boyfriend and your father have been pulling. So, I'm not expecting you to have answers, or to need anything or to do anything. I just want to let you know that, ... well, we were friends once."

"We still are," she stated.

He smiled and nodded. "Certainly, considering what you're doing, and I really appreciate it."

Her shoulders sagged, as she added, "It's one of the hardest things I've ever done."

He paid the bill and they got up to walk outside.

She looked at his truck and said, "Please tell me that's paid for."

"It is," he replied cheerfully. "She won't be getting that."

"They might put a lien on it to sell against other debts or something."

He shrugged. "We'll try to do something about it if it comes to that," he noted. "Still, they would have to prove that they're my debts."

"But they were made in your name."

"I'm not going there right now," he declared. "I have to believe in things turning out the right way. Otherwise it will be one more injustice that I'll really struggle with, and I don't need any more of that right now."

"No, of course not," she agreed. "I'm sorry about all that."

# CHAPTER 6

BURKE GAVE SHIRLEY a hug and hopped into his truck, then waited until she was in her car and had pulled away. She drove a small older car. She had always made decent money, and he had meant to talk to her about that, but then they got completely sidetracked. He pulled out his phone and called her.

"That didn't take long." She chuckled.

"We forgot to set up a game plan for tomorrow. What are you doing about your bank accounts and all that?"

"I've already figured out what I need to do," she replied, with a sigh. "Not a whole lot I can do but show up at the bank tomorrow on my lunch hour."

"Do you think that's soon enough?"

"I hope so." She hesitated, then asked, "You're really worried, aren't you?"

"Yes, because, with my credit cards blocked, and their not having anything else set up yet, if they find out that you had anything to do with it, you'll become target number one. I know you don't want to do it, but I would phone tonight and at least get your credit cards canceled."

"Ouch."

"And if you have any recurring charges, confirm you let them know that."

"I will," she said, "thanks for that."

"I'm sorry." And he found himself repeating the apology before hanging up.

He drove slowly back home, worried about her and about the whole scenario. When he pulled in to the Haven, Timber was sitting out on the deck, a pad of paper in his hands. Burke walked up slowly and greeted him. "Hey."

Timber held up a hand, which in their world always meant *freeze*.

Burke froze, and, as he watched, an armadillo on the back deck was a few steps away from where Timber sat, then looked back at Timber before moving along the deck to the grassy area. "Good God," Burke murmured. "Are all animals welcome?"

"All animals are welcome," Timber declared.

"What was wrong with him?"

"He had some plastic tied around his neck."

"Tied on purpose?"

"No, more like garbage that had gotten tangled around his neck, and he wanted it taken off," he clarified, with a smile. "Job accomplished."

"Wow," he muttered.

"How are you doing?" Timber asked.

"I'm okay. I just talked to the cops, then ended up having dinner with Shirley."

"How did that go?"

Burke frowned. "In a way it was very emotional for both of us because we have known each other for a while, and this involves her family, so it's not an easy thing for either one of us to handle right now."

"That's got to be tough," Timber replied.

"Absolutely, yet it's what it is, so what can I do?"

Timber smiled. "You do what you're doing, and, with

that, you just keep on going because what else can you do?"

"That's what I was thinking," Burke agreed, with half a laugh. "It's just frustrating to see good people getting hit all the time."

"And that's exactly what's happening to you. It's frustrating for us to watch this too because we don't know how to help either."

"I'm hoping, after talking to the lawyer today, that maybe we can find an easy solution to this. The credit card companies have frozen everything, and, according to Shirley, Silvia's quite pissed because she's already aware that the cards can no longer be used."

"Of course, since, as soon as you freeze those credit cards, she's suddenly out of funds."

"Shirley did say that Silvia has three cards in my name. I'm hoping that all of them are now canceled, but I don't know for sure. So I'll have to talk to Gregory about that."

"Who is Gregory?"

"Tommy's friend, the digital PI."

"That would be a good thing to do now."

"She'll also freeze her cards tonight too."

"Shirley will?" he asked.

"Yeah, and maybe that's overkill, but ..."

"But what?"

"I just have a really ugly feeling that, if Silvia can't access the credit cards in my name—and doesn't have access to somebody else's cards set up yet to steal from—Silvia likely already knows about her sister's credit cards. So, if she finds out Shirley turned them in—"

"Her sister becomes free game," Timber added, "and you're right. From what I've heard about your ex-girlfriend, Silvia would do that."

"That's the thing. Shirley also has some money in the bank that she saved from when she did project management work, and, since her sister has been at her place, Silvia could very well have information on all those accounts."

"Oh, crap."

"Yeah, and, of course, the banks are now closed however there is an emergency number to call right now. And  she needs to go there first thing in the morning."

"I think so too."

"She needs to change accounts and change debit cards. Everything."

"Do you think she needs to change banks as well?"

Timber grimaced. "I would change banks, just in case. You don't know if she's got somebody helping her. These con artists are able to access things they shouldn't be able to all the time, so somebody has to be helping them."

"That's a scary thought too. I'll warn her about that." He pulled out his phone and quickly texted her to share Timber's suggestions. When his phone rang, he asked, "Hey, did you make it home okay?"

"I made it home," she shared. "And I just got off the phone with the credit card companies. I canceled all my cards."

"That's good to know."

"What's this about changing banks?"

He put it on Speaker and stated, "I've got Timber here beside me. It was his suggestion that you should probably change banks, not just accounts, because—depending on how your sister and this guy are operating—they could have help on the inside."

"Jesus. That means I need to go there first thing in the morning."

"I would have suggested you do that anyway," Timber interjected. "If she's now running out of money, she'll find it somewhere, and you know she won't start looking for a job at this stage of the game. So, she'll go for the easiest money. Plus, if she thinks that you owe her in some way, it won't be much of a stretch to take it from you, especially if she's getting pressure from the guy in her life."

Burke asked, "How far of a stretch is it for her to decide that you owe her, and she could go collect some of it right now?"

"Not much of a stretch at all."

"And, if she had access to your account, she might just take a little bit out from an ATM machine. However, if she finds out how much is in there, she might decide that the best avenue would be to drain it."

"From an ATM, she would see the balance, and I don't know if she could take all of it, but I wouldn't be happy if she took any of it," she grumbled. "I have a lot of money locked up in savings or investments."

"Are they all through the same bank?" Timber asked.

"No," she replied thoughtfully, "that was closer to my old location."

"As in an investment account?"

"Yes."

"Then I suggest you contact them and have them put a fraud alert on your account, so they're to be extra vigilant."

"Can I do that?"

"Yes, you can," he declared.

She muttered, "I guess I'm making phone calls now and going to work late in the morning."

"Will you lose your job over that?"

"I would hope not," she replied, "but no point in going to work on time to save my job only to allow my sister to clean out my money, especially since this job would never allow me to earn that kind of money back. Jeez, that came out a little convoluted," she confessed, "but basically …"

"It's okay," Burke interrupted. "We got it."

"Right. … Damn, I want to do something about it right now, but I don't know what."

"You could start with emails to the investment company. They may even have a twenty-four-hour phone number for fraud alerts."

"Oh, good idea, I didn't think of that."

"And, whatever time your bank opens in the morning, be there early. Take all your cards and make sure, whatever you decide to do, that you come away with new accounts and clean cards, and add all the extra security that you can."

"I can try that too," she muttered, "but, if you expect me to sleep now, that's not happening."

"No, of course not."

She disconnected soon afterward.

As they sat here after the call, Timber asked, "You really care about her, don't you?"

"I definitely care, though it's not something I've had a chance to think about," he noted cautiously. "I don't want you to read anything into it just yet, but obviously she's done something huge for me."

"Yes, she has," he agreed, "and I'm really happy that we are at this stage of it so fast."

"In that family, Shirley was always the nice one."

"Good enough." Timber chuckled. "Yet I highly suspect something is there."

"Yeah, I think there probably is," he admitted, with a sly smile. "However, I wasn't exactly thinking along those lines right now."

"No, but maybe you should be."

Burke studied his friend.

Timber nodded and continued. "I did the same thing, you know? I wanted to wait, to see if something else, *somebody* else, showed any interest, or maybe just wait for a better time," he shared. "It was always about time for me. I wanted somebody in my life, but I was thinking that would be good, *after* I got the refuge set up, *after* I got a house fixed, *after* I got all kinds of things done. Then I would look for somebody." Timber shook his head. "Suddenly there she was, and, like everything else around here, it took on a life of its own. So I now feel a whole lot better knowing that I'm in a committed relationship, and I'm not even worried about all that now," he shared. "She's perfect for my life."

"And she was supposed to come with the horses today?"

"No, another vet, who couldn't make it. Tiffany will be here for the receiving. So, it worked out better anyway because Tiffany was crazy busy at her practice over the past few days."

"That's good to hear it worked out." Burke smiled at his buddy. "At least you don't feel quite so bad, as long as the horses are being cared for where they are."

"And they are, but they'll be here tomorrow."

"Good enough. I want to be here too, if I don't have to go back to town and deal with this other stuff."

"Yeah, but if you do, you do," Timber said. "This place isn't just about the animals, it's about everybody." He smiled.

Burke agreed. "I really like the fact that you do include the animals in this."

"The animals are the reason I'm doing this, and I can see that very quickly we'll probably end up overwhelmed in numbers, but that's okay too."

"It's absolutely okay," Burke agreed. "You have a lot of land here to develop."

"I know, and now that I've got all the acreage, I'll go out with Andy soon and start sorting out the marker lines, property corner markers, and all that, so I can get it fenced. Apparently some of it is fenced, and that's a good thing, but an awful lot of acreage is here that I need to look after."

"And is it land that you need to look after?" Burke asked cautiously. "Or is it land that will look after itself?"

"Both," Timber clarified, "and, because of the problems that we had originally, I won't assume that it'll look after itself. I'll need to keep an eye on it, and I also want to get to know the land, so that I understand exactly what's here. That includes the watering hole that Andy told me is here because that water is everything. So, if we end up with other kinds of issues, we want to ensure something is available for everybody."

"And, of course, we don't know how good of a watering hole it is yet."

"No, we don't," he stated cheerfully, "but the fact we have a watering hole is a good start, and we'll take the next step and figure it out."

As Burke sat beside Timber on the deck, the call of an owl came from somewhere in the bush. Timber lifted his hands and made a call right back again. Burke watched in amazement as a huge horned owl swooped in and landed on the railing beside him.

Timber chuckled. "Hey, Gibraltar. How are you doing tonight?"

A weird chuckling sound came from the back of the bird's throat, and he leaned forward, his gaze focused on Burke.

"Good God," Burke muttered in amazement.

"Yeah, this guy came in with a busted wing a while back. I didn't even have this place yet. I was just out wandering around, looking at the land, trying to figure out whether I should buy it or not when I found him. It was one of those moments when you truly realize that this is where you belong. This guy came right up to me, and I managed to splint his wing and gave him a chunk of leftover steak I had in my sandwich with me at the time, and we've been fast friends ever since," he explained, with a smile. "It always does my heart good to have him come say hi."

"The fact that I'm here with you, and he still came up," Burke noted, "is huge. I would love to touch him, but I don't know that he would trust me."

"He's a good judge of character though," Timber replied.

As Burke held out his hand for the huge owl to access it, he shared, "I feel as if he's wondering if my hand is edible."

"And he might be considering it," Timber noted, with a laugh. "Never had a problem with it, but that doesn't mean he won't decide that would make a tasty meal. And don't kid yourself. That beak of his could take off a finger in a heartbeat."

As Burke continued to hold out his hand steadily, the owl walked a little bit closer, not taking his gaze off Burke. "Good God, he's unbelievably beautiful." The owl seemed to be taking the measure of Burke.

"Isn't he? He's so majestic, and he is so much just himself. I think that's the joy of animals. It's … they're them. They don't try to be anything else. They are just happy being who they are. I don't think they even think about changing who they are," Timber offered, with a smile.

The owl stayed for a long time, and finally he cocked his head to one side and suddenly lifted up, those huge powerful wings beating in the air, as he slowly rose and circled above.

"Now he'll be hunting," Timber whispered.

"And for him to live, another animal has to die."

Timber looked over at Burke and nodded slowly. "It's the circle of life, and, as much as I understand and accept that, it still hurts sometimes."

"Of course, because we want everybody to live in peace and harmony, but nobody ever does," Burke noted, with a wry smile.

"Some of us do, but, in the animal kingdom, not so much." And he left that thought hanging.

"Anyway, I'm off to bed," Burke announced, as he got up. "I just wanted to thank you again for letting me stay here."

Timber turned to him. "Why the hell would you even bring that up?" he asked, his voice rusty. "You know very well that you're always welcome here."

"I know, and, for that, I thank you even more because … just knowing that, no matter what, I have a place to call home, a haven for me, … is huge."

"And that's the correct use of the word *haven*," Timber pointed out. "Remember that … you're not alone."

# CHAPTER 7

S HIRLEY WAS OUTSIDE the bank when it opened that next morning, and, as she walked in, she looked around, hating that same nervousness, wondering if her sister knew. If Silvia already knew about Shirley's money, an unpleasant surprise was coming Silvia's way. Shirley really hoped she had been fast enough, but Timber had started that feeling of not panic, but, well, maybe panic.

As she got to the teller, she checked her account balances and quickly asked for a money order to remove it all.

The teller stared at her. "We can give you a draft, and you can take it, but why would you want to? We're looking after your money just fine, aren't we?"

"Yes, but because of some issues involving fraud with somebody I know, someone who has had access to my account information, I'm just not comfortable leaving the money here."

The teller continued to stare at her. "But they can't get into your account."

"It doesn't matter. I'm not willing to argue about this, and, for my own peace of mind, I want to move my money," she stated firmly.

The teller made a strange sound, a shadow crossing her face, then replied, "I am sorry for the inconvenience, but I'll have to talk to the manager about it."

Shirley's eyebrows shot up, and she stated, "It's my money."

"Yes, it is your money," she began apologetically, "but the fact is, it's more money than we're used to dealing with at one time."

"Then you need to deal with it now," Shirley stated. This seemed to be working against her. "I don't have time for this. I need to get to work too."

"You can also come back another day."

"Let me talk to the manager," she declared.

The teller shrugged. "I'll see if he's available."

As soon as she left, Shirley turned around, feeling some strange gazes on her, and yet the bank was basically empty of customers. Still, it just felt off. She sighed.

When the teller returned, she said, "He'll see you now."

Shirley nodded and was led into a small office.

The bank manager looked at her with a kindly smile and asked, "Now, what's the problem?"

"The problem is, I want to move my money to another bank," she declared.

"Why?"

To avoid a really long and unnecessary discussion about her decision regarding her own damn account, she stated, "I want to do this, and it's my money, and you can't talk me out of it." He frowned at her, and she shook her head. "No, you're not, and please do not give me any more trouble about this."

"You do have to give us a certain amount of time."

"I'm not asking for cash," she clarified. "I'm asking for a money order." He frowned at that. "Don't tell me that you can't do that because obviously you can. You move money all the time."

"Sure," he replied. "We could move it, but that's a dicier way of doing it."

"In what way?" she asked.

"You don't want to carry that cash around."

"I didn't say cash. I specifically said a *money order.*" Then she frowned at him. "Are you trying to stop me from doing this? Are you in cahoots with somebody over this?"

He looked at her and shook his head. "No, … no, … of course not."

She frowned at him. "Yet you're really working hard to try to stop me from moving my own money."

"We never want to see money leave the bank," he explained. "Surely that's not hard to understand."

"It might not be hard to understand," she stated, "but I insist on this, and I don't appreciate the pushback."

"Fine," he said.

It took another twenty minutes for them to get it settled. When Shirley finally walked out of there with a bank draft in her pocket, she felt even more unnerved and leery about carrying that money, and yet it was supposedly secure.

She had chosen another bank a little bit farther away, and she quickly got into her vehicle. As she drove away, she swore she saw her sister walking up to the bank, and, with that, she started to shake. As far as she knew, Silvia had never used the same bank as her.

But now that all the money was gone and her accounts closed, Shirley wanted to confirm that this wouldn't be an issue. She drove quickly, wondering what bank to use, which one her sister would not expect, and which was the most secure. Then she found herself phoning Burke to ask him.

He quickly gave her the name of a bank that had branches across the country, with one of the best reputations.

She looked it up on her GPS, found one close by. Feeling a sense of relief, she drove into the parking lot and, within minutes, had new accounts, new cards, and her money safely deposited.

The manager looked at her and noted, "You seem quite relieved over that."

"I am," she confirmed. "When you find out that family members have had access to your cards and are in bad financial straits and don't have any morals, you worry about them going in and cleaning out your accounts."

The other woman winced. "We don't want that to ever happen."

"Are there any extra checks or alerts you can put on my accounts to confirm nobody else can access this money?"

"Sure," she replied, "we can add some extra features." And, with that, they settled on a couple that would give Shirley a little bit more security. "You're really worried, aren't you?"

"I am," she confirmed, "and I know it may be foolish—"

"No, it's not foolish. Sometimes, as much as we don't want to, it's the only answer, and, if it's family, you are stuck between a rock and a hard place."

"We don't always want everybody to know how much money we have, particularly when we work, and they don't," Shirley explained.

"Oh, that's even worse," the nice teller muttered. "I don't understand that sense of entitlement, where they just feel as if, because you have what they want, they can just reach out and take it."

Shirley sighed and nodded. "And that's the attitude exactly, with absolutely no sense of right or wrong, of their having what they shouldn't have, with no care for others. If they had any idea I had this money, I am convinced they would do everything they could to take it."

"Did you just clean out an account somewhere?"

"I did," she confessed. "My sister has been in my home, has seen my mail, my purse, my cards, so who knows what information she might have been collecting. As of yesterday, she was reported and will be getting into big trouble, and it was suggested that I move my accounts."

"That was a very wise thing to do. And now I've put an alert on this one, in case anybody even tries to access it that isn't you," she shared. "As usual, you'll have to watch the activity on your cards, and, should you see any odd transactions, you need to let us know."

"Will do, and the credit card company as well."

"Right, now they will call you if there's a certain number of transactions that look odd to them, but that doesn't mean they'll catch them all."

"Of course not, and thank you." Shirley headed out and went to work. As she walked into her job and sat at her desk, she found a phone call message from her sister on her cell phone.

She stared down at her phone, but her boss walked up. "I know you told me that you would be an hour late," he began, "but it's been an hour and a half already."

She winced. "I'm so sorry. I'll work hard to get through the line-ups."

"Well"—he shrugged—"please stay and make up for the lost time. We're really short-staffed right now, so pitch in."

And, with that, she put down her own phone and got to work. The last thing she needed was to lose her job. So far, she had been very good about making sure that absolutely nothing could be held against her as a black mark, and the one thing she did not need right now was her sister causing trouble too.

And considering Shirley may have seen Silvia going into the bank this morning, it was possible Silvia was calling about that, and Shirley definitely didn't want to talk to her.

When her lunchtime came around, instead of taking it, she worked right through, noting the approval on her manager's face, even though she wouldn't get paid for it. It was a small price to pay for keeping her job, which, whether she needed it or not at this point, she didn't know. But it was one more issue she didn't want to deal with. She already needed to move and didn't know where to go, but to maintain this job with her sister knowing where she worked meant that her sister would be coming here to find her—especially if Shirley moved—and that was the last thing Shirley wanted.

Speaking of Silvia showing up at Shirley's job, it was even a possibility here and now. If her sister did that and made a scene, it would be the end of Shirley's job. Just the thought was enough to make Shirley cringe. When her day was finally done, and she'd worked the extra hours that she needed to make up for her appointment this morning, she stood with a heavy sigh. The manager walked over and asked, "Are you okay?"

"Sure," she replied. "It was just a longer day than I had planned."

"Of course, but we appreciate the fact that you made up for the lost time."

She nodded. "I'm so sorry for being later than I expected this morning."

He accepted the apology and added, "Let's just hope it doesn't happen again."

"I hope not."

"Also … somebody was stopped outside today, asking if you were at work."

"What?" she asked in horror. "Who?"

"You've been a great employee, and we really don't want to lose you. But, if any personal problem ends up coming to the office, you do realize," he explained somewhat apologetically, "that would result in an instant dismissal."

She stared at him and asked, "But it hasn't happened though, right?"

"No, it hasn't, but, if this person becomes a problem, you need to stop them from coming back and causing trouble …"

"Did they cause trouble today?" she asked.

"No, just a minor disturbance. Again … I'm just being cautious."

It seemed as if he was being *more than* cautious, yet he didn't have any reason for that criticism and made her feel almost targeted. "Thank you for letting me know," she replied.

And, with that, she walked out, feeling as if everything in her world was about to collapse, and she didn't have a clue how to stop it, or if she even could.

# CHAPTER 8

B URKE DIDN'T HEAR from Shirley yesterday, hoping she made it to the bank on time. So, when he woke up the next morning, a sense of unease crawled under his skin, probably because of these unpleasant financial circumstances surrounding Silvia and his concerns for Shirley. He got out of bed, dressed quickly, and walked downstairs and into the kitchen. Dwight was already cooking, coffee already on, but Burke saw no sign of anybody else.

As soon as he walked toward the front porch, a low-pitched warning came from Timber. Burke slowed his steps until he gingerly came out onto the front porch and saw the doe and her fawn, eating the little bits of grass off to the side of the front yard. It was the first time he'd seen them this close. Just watching both mom and baby—happy, free, and content—made him smile.

Timber lifted a hand and pointed in a different direction. Burke froze. A black bear had his back up against one of the huge posts they'd put up to run hydro lines. The bear was completely unconcerned as he worked his back against the post, as if to scratch an itch.

Burke quickly sat down beside both Toby and Timber. "Don't tell me that he's another one you rescued."

Timber chuckled. "No, but he's been coming around a lot."

"Is that good or bad?"

Timber shrugged. "I won't say either way at this point, but, as long as he hasn't caused any chaos, we're fine."

Toby inclined his head toward the bear. "We call him Big Mike."

Timber added, "He's not after anybody here, and he's not causing any trouble, so I'm good with him popping by for a visit, since it goes along with everything else that we're doing here."

"I guess. It's not as if he needs help, right?" Burke asked.

"No, not at the moment anyway. But I do want him to come if he does need help, and that means he needs to be comfortable here." Timber studied the bear intently.

At that, the bear dropped down to all four legs, wandered around a little bit, sensed them up on the front porch, but, instead of walking away, he stopped to look at them. Then he slowly meandered around the yard, before finally disappearing out of sight.

"Beautiful animal," Burke whispered.

Timber smiled and nodded. "That's one of the reasons I want to keep this land up here."

"Of course, it's their land too."

"Exactly," he agreed, with a note of satisfaction. He looked over at him and asked, "Did you get any sleep?"

"I got some. Nothing quite like having my identity stolen to further steal from me, while I've got other things happening right now, to pull my strings and to wake me up. I seem to be thinking about the worst-case scenario of everything that can go wrong."

"Of course," Timber noted, with a smile, "but hopefully you'll also have some good things to think about."

"I haven't heard anything from Shirley today—or yesterday," he shared, with a worried look on his face. "I texted her, but I'm not sure she got the message."

"She's probably not up and awake yet either."

"No, … probably not," he conceded, "but I would feel better if she had sent me a note to say she was doing okay."

"Then reach out again and ask her."

He pondered that for a moment, then did exactly that. "Hope I didn't wake her up."

"Depends on what time she starts work," Timber noted, his voice still mellow from watching the bear.

When Burke's phone buzzed, he looked down and nodded. "She's awake." Then he smiled and shared, "She went to the bank yesterday, removed the money, and set up a new account and got new cards, all with extra alerts set up."

"That's good news," Timber noted.

When Burke's cell buzzed again, he frowned. "Shirley thinks she saw Silvia heading into her bank immediately afterward." He started texting back, asking if Silvia had accounts there. "As far as she knows, her sister never had an account there, but Shirley can't be sure. So now she's worried Silvia was there trying to get to Shirley's money."

"That seems understandable and would be my first thought too."

"Yep, mine too."

"Of course, now that Shirley knows what her family has been up to, it will be hard to stay neutral."

"I don't even think she can stay neutral, not with cooperating with the police and realizing she's at risk herself," he added.

At that, Timber nodded. "Yet Shirley doesn't have a whole lot of options when it comes to that level of deceit and fraudulent activity."

"It's certainly appreciated on my end," Burke shared. "I just hope it doesn't have repercussions for her."

Dwight stepped out with a coffeepot and topped up their cups. "Now that we have the wildlife becoming as active as they are, we've got to keep the garbage contained around here."

Timber looked at him and then slowly nodded. "Good point. Is there something more we need to do?" he asked, as he looked around at his property. "I would have thought we had most of it contained."

"Most of it maybe," Dwight conceded. "But most of it isn't all of it. We just need to give the guys a heads-up. Breakfast won't be long." With that, he headed back inside with the coffeepot.

Burke looked over at Timber. "He really likes doing the cooking, doesn't he?"

"He seems to. When he first got here, he was out there swinging a hammer with the rest of us, but very quickly he decided to use his skills inside, and he's been a godsend."

"He alone?"

"Yeah, mostly. Toby here is a hell of a cook too, and helps out when needed."

"Of course, it's not easy feeding us all."

All at once their day started rather abruptly, as a big trailer came down the driveway while they were eating. "I wasn't expecting them quite yet," Timber muttered, as he stood up.

"What is it?" Toby asked, putting down the tongs and stepping outside.

"It looks as if the horses are here."

"What about intake?"

"Let's hope Tiffany was given a better word about timing than I was," Timber noted. "I'll give her a call in a few minutes." But, sure enough, driving behind the trailer was Tiffany.

She pulled up and parked, then walked over to the driver's side of the delivery vehicle and directed him to where she wanted the trailer parked. As they got turned around and backed it up, she walked over, gave Timber a big hug, then looked at Burke and smiled. "Are you settling in pretty well?" she asked in a teasing voice.

"A little too well maybe," he replied, with a smile.

"Oh, now that's easy to do here," she noted. "It's a peaceful place to begin with. Then with the added opportunity to help set up a situation that will be so good for both the animals and the people who come through," she added, "it's pretty hard to not want to pitch in and do something." He just nodded. Then she walked back over to the driver with the horses, where they had a long discussion and started going over the paperwork.

She returned to join Timber and said, "I can take care of some of the paperwork, but the rest will require your input and signature."

Burke got up and walked over to join them, as they discussed the horses. When they were ready to unload, he opened up the big gates, then opened up the back of the trailer, and started leading the horses out, one by one. Some of them were in okay shape, a couple rather desperately needed farrier work, and one was limping pretty badly.

He wasn't sure whether it was the fetlock, the hoof, or something else. One of the other ones was skin and bones. He paused when he looked at her and whispered, "So sorry, sweetheart. We'll get you fixed up."

By the time he had them unloaded, he turned around to

find Timber going over each animal's condition with Tiffany.

She smiled at Burke. "You're obviously used to horses."

"I am," he confirmed, with a gentle smile. "God's creatures."

She nodded. "But then I think all of them are God's creatures."

He laughed. "I won't argue the point, but horses definitely have a soft spot in my heart."

"That's not a bad thing," she noted. "If you want to give me a hand, we'll move a couple over so I can start checkups. I want to record some stats for them and see just what kind of problems we've got." She motioned toward her vehicle. "I brought a portable X-ray scanner with me too," she shared.

When he raised one eyebrow, she nodded. "It's one of those investments that you make, not sure if you really need to, but you do it because you want it."

The next two hours were spent leading each horse into one of the treatment areas, where she did a thorough check of them, wrote down notes as to what they needed, and then they were separated. Most went straight to a couple pastures, where they were happy to be left alone to do their own thing. A few of them she kept in one of the paddocks up close.

Burke asked her, "Do you have a farrier?"

"No, I'll have to call somebody in."

He hesitated but added, "Look. I'm not licensed, but I've done plenty of it." When she looked at him, he shrugged. "My uncle had a farm, and he was a farrier by trade."

"In that case, until we can get somebody in, do you want to give us a hand to make these two a little more comfortable? They've got very overgrown and cracked hooves."

"I saw that," he noted. "It's one of the reasons I offered. I'll have to get some tools though," he pointed out. "That's something I didn't bring with me."

She nodded. "Do you want to make a trip to town?"

He winced. "Not really."

She burst out laughing at that. Tommy soon came over and announced that he was heading into town to get supplies and asked if anybody needed anything.

She smiled at him. "You might be sorry you asked."

He laughed. "Probably, but, in a place like this, we always need somebody to go pick up stuff. I've already got a list of groceries to pick up for Dwight, plus the list from the building crew. So, what do you need?"

She was on the phone quickly, and, once she confirmed they had the tools, she set it up so Tommy could just go by and pick them up.

"That's great, thanks." He looked over at Burke. "You want to come for a ride?"

"No thanks, I'll stay here and help with the horses," he replied.

"You do that," Tommy muttered. "Horses aren't my thing. I like them from a distance, but I don't feel like getting too close." He frowned as he watched one horse eye him nervously. "It's almost as if they hear me."

"They do," she confirmed, "and they know exactly who's afraid of them and who's not."

"Which in itself is creepy," Tommy muttered. "That's why I'm better with a hammer or a computer." Then he gave them a smile and added, "You guys look after the horses. I'll give my back a break and do a town run."

"Sounds good."

And, with that, he was up and off fairly quickly.

Tiffany looked over at Burke. "Are you okay to give me a hand for another hour or two?"

"Sure." He watched in amazement as she thoroughly but gently worked on the worst two horses, building up a nutritional panel for the one and X-rayed the injured leg on the other.

She muttered, "It's not broken. So that's a good thing, but it's definitely inflamed. So, we'll see what we can do about that."

"What is it then?"

"Hopefully just a sprain," she suggested, waving her hand. "We'll need to wrap it for support and give her some meds, and hopefully it won't be too uncomfortable when you work on her hooves."

"We can bind it now to get a start on the hoof, once I get the tools," he noted.

Together they worked for another couple hours. When she finally sat back, she sighed. "Okay. I think that's all we can do for today, at least until the tools arrive."

He nodded. "It shouldn't be too long now, should it?"

"It's hard to say, depending on what all Tommy had to pick up," she said, with a laugh. "I would love to get a start on it today, but, if we can't, we can't."

Just then Timber walked in, and the horse nickered at him. He walked over and spent a few minutes just talking to her. She relaxed completely against him, dropping her head down to blow air gently down his neck. He smiled up at the mare. "You'll be just fine, honest. We just need to get some tools, and we'll get you fixed up." She nickered softly, and he just kept talking to her, his voice calm and completely natural. But then that was Timber.

Burke smiled at him. "This really is where you belong,

isn't it?"

He nodded. "Yes, and the good news is, I know it," he declared, with a big smile. "So, I'm not planning on going anywhere, just working to get horses and other animals, like this one, where they need to be." He looked over at Tiffany. "What's the verdict?"

"It's not broken," she said, "so that's the good news. Burke will get her trimmed up. Then we'll bind it, wrap it up, and give her a little bit more support until it heals."

"And the other one?" he asked.

"We'll get her nutrition panel fixed up, and her diet will have to be modified. From the looks of it, she's extremely weak and worn down. She's in need of a trim as well, so getting that done will make her more comfortable and will encourage her to move around a bit more."

He nodded and didn't say anything.

Burke looked at him and shared, "You seem to be handling all this pretty easily."

"There'll be an awful lot worse that we'll see as time goes on," he pointed out. "We'll just deal with what we can, never quite knowing what will show up next." He looked over at Tiffany, "I came to tell you that there's coffee."

"Coffee would be good," she said.

He laughed. "Coffee is always good, even if you do drink too much."

She rolled her eyes at him. "Hardly."

He wrapped an arm around her shoulders and led her back up to the house, turning to look at Burke. "There's coffee on, if you want some too."

"Yeah, I'll come in a few," Burke replied. "I will just visit with this gal for a bit."

"Go ahead. Just remember she's had her heart broken a

time or two."

"I know, and she's showing it. Nothing quite like people who treat them like tools instead of family."

"I know," Timber muttered. "That's another reason why I'm trying to bring as many here as I can."

As soon as they were out of the room, he moved over and gently stroked the older mare's neck, giving her time to get used to him and his touch. She had shied away initially but seemed to be more accepting now.

"Nobody here will hurt you, sweetheart," he vowed. "I know you don't believe me yet, but you will. Soon enough you will. And, when those tools get here, we'll see if we can get you walking a little easier."

She had completely overgrown hooves, and one was cracked. It broke his heart to see animals in this condition, but people were people.

As he walked back to the cabin to get coffee, Tommy drove up, honking the horn, as he went to cross the yard.

Heading for the truck instead of coffee, Burke asked, "Were you able to get the tools?"

"Sure did," he confirmed, as he handed them off. "Tiffany had it all set up for me."

"That's good."

Tommy laughed. "Better you have them than me. I can't imagine those horses will be that happy to have you using these tools on them at this point in time."

"It's hard to say," he admitted. "Their hooves are pretty overgrown and cracked. Yet, after I'm done with them, this will make them feel a lot better."

"If you say so." Tommy shook his head. "As long as it helps."

Tommy then backed the truck up toward the building

where the construction crew had been working. Several of them came out to help unload whatever else he'd picked up, but Burke had his farrier tools in hand and headed to have a look at the mare's hooves. He would rather fix these up first, then go for coffee.

Completely focused on the task at hand, he settled into it right away. Before long, he straightened up and patted the mare. "That should do it. How does that feel?" he asked the mare.

"Seems to be a whole lot better than it was."

He looked over to see Tiffany, smiling at him. "That was a nice job."

He shrugged. "As I told you, I'm not formally trained," he cautioned, "as in I'm not certified or anything."

"Nope, and I hear you. Lots of things that we do in life we do because we learned how, but that doesn't mean we have any credentials or certification," she stated, with a becoming smile. "My father was like that. He was incredibly capable and didn't have certificates for most things, but we still got along just fine."

"What did he do?" he asked.

"A whole lot of everything and a whole lot of nothing," she replied, with a chuckle. Just then the horse nickered, and somebody out in the pasture nickered back. "That's her saying she wants to go join the others, now that she can walk a bit better," she shared, as she led her over to the paddock gate, where she opened it wide and let the mare out. As soon as the mare cautiously stepped through and then realized a big open field was in front of her, she picked up the pace and started to move toward the others.

"She looks pretty happy, doesn't she?" Burke asked.

"She does, indeed," Tiffany agreed, with a smile. "She'll

be just fine. Thank you for doing that."

He stared at the horses, absolutely loving the fact that Timber was helping them. Burke realized that he wanted to do something similar, but he didn't know exactly what. Just that he wanted to do something with meaning.

As he stood here, Tiffany tapped him on the shoulder, "That's an odd look on your face."

"Not so odd," he muttered, with a sad smile. "Just the realization that I very much want to be doing something similar."

"Similar to what? To what Timber is doing?"

"Yeah, similar in the sense that he's helping people and helping animals."

"Good," she stated. "A lot of room for it. While you're here, you might as well figure out what he's doing, and maybe he needs help with something specific."

Burke nodded, listening intently.

She hesitated, adding, "I hope you don't mind, but he did tell me a little bit about the troubles you're having."

"*Yeah*, and that is having an impact on me deciding my next move because I don't know if I'll be on the hook for this mess in terms of finances."

"You shouldn't be, but ..."

"Exactly. It's the *but* part that's hard to live with."

She smiled. "I have faith that things will turn out well."

"I do too," he conceded, and he really did. He didn't know why, but he was feeling hopeful that it would all work out in his favor. As he went to go grab coffee, his phone rang. He looked down and realized it was Shirley. "Hey, Shirley. How are you doing?" But there was a sob on the other end. "Are you okay? What happened?" He could tell that she had obviously been crying.

"I got laid off at work today, so I can't say I'm doing very well."

"What? Why?" he asked.

"Silvia. … She came to my office today and absolutely lost it on me."

"Why?" But inside he already knew the answer.

"Because she couldn't access my money," she shared. "I had been warned yesterday that somebody had been outside the office trying to get in to see me and that, if my personal life caused disruptions at work, I could be dismissed, but I didn't really think too much about it as I didn't have any reason to think she would go so completely haywire."

"But she did?"

"She did, and I got sacked for it."

"That won't help her either then, will it? So she did try to get money out of your bank account then?"

"Yes. She told me that I owed her and was furious because I had taken what she called *her* money. Of course my bosses weren't interested in hearing the truth of the matter. They just didn't want any disturbance, so guess who was asked to leave?"

She laughed hysterically. "Honestly, I can't believe this happened," she muttered, sniffling back tears, "but now I'm unemployed, and I'm walking around my apartment, knowing that I'll have to leave this too, with no idea what my best move is at the moment. But the reality is that Silvia will be here soon enough. I'm sure of it."

"Do you have much?"

"No, I don't, honestly. She destroyed a lot of it the last time she threw a fit, and then, when I went away for a holiday with some girlfriends from school, Silvia supposedly left the door unlocked, and I got robbed. So, I've been living with the bare minimum for a while now."

"So, knowing what you now know about your sister, do you think you got robbed or do you think she was the one who robbed you?"

A long sigh came, and she replied, "I don't even want to think about that, but it's possible."

"Of course it's possible," he stated, with a groan. "I'm so sorry."

"Yeah, me too," she muttered. "Right now, I'm just exhausted and worn out. My rent is due, and I'll be okay for a while as, thankfully, I do have money. I just can't stay here right now. I want to avoid Silvia when she is this mad."

"I can understand that."

"Not after what she just did. Plus, I know she'll be coming after me," she pointed out, "maybe even with that scary boyfriend of hers. So I am not sure where and what I'm doing at the moment."

He didn't know what to say, but Timber piped up, "If that's Shirley, and she's in trouble, tell her to come here."

"Do you have room for her though?" Burke asked.

"There's a spare bedroom upstairs. She can come and figure out what she wants to do from here," Timber offered. "She helped you out, so let's help her out."

At that, Burke spoke into the phone, "Did you hear what Timber just said?"

"I did," she whispered, "but I don't want to be in the way. I don't really have any reason to come out there, and I don't want to stop all the work you guys are doing."

Timber grabbed the phone and gave her directions, completely overriding her objections. "A bedroom is here for you, so don't be foolish. When you get offered an opportunity, you take it," he stated. "Let's confirm your sister won't find you right now."

"That would be a big help." And there was no mistaking the tremor of tears in her voice.

"Do we know if she has heard anything about the pending court case or the detective's investigation?"

"I wouldn't think so, but I honestly don't know. She's been calling me, but, especially after I lost my job. ... I haven't felt like answering."

"Good and don't," Timber stated. "If you can get away, ... then get away. I don't know what you have to pack up, but ... Are you on a lease?"

"No, it's month-to-month."

"In that case you know what you need to do," he declared, with a hint of sharpness. "Put whatever you care about in your vehicle and get away from there."

"I don't even have anything to care about left," she explained. "I haven't even been cooking here. After everything got completely wiped out, I basically just moved the little that was left."

"Then give up your apartment, tell your landlord you're done, and get your ass over here. We'll figure out what's next." Then he gave her the signpost to turn at.

She hesitated. "Are you sure?"

"I know you don't know me, so you don't know that's almost an insult to ask me that. However, I am sure, so come on. Let's sort this out from here," he added. "We don't want you to have a run-in with your sister, especially with that boyfriend."

"Oh God," she muttered. "I'm already throwing shit into my suitcase."

"Do you need a hand?" he asked.

"No, I don't have much," she shared, panic in her voice.

"And now you've put the fear of God in me at the thought of him showing up with her."

"That bad?" Timber asked, his voice hard.

Tiffany's hand landed on his shoulder as she listened in.

"Yeah," Shirley replied, "that bad."

"Maybe I should come then," Burke interjected.

"No," Shirley said immediately. "If they see you, it'll be an all-out war."

"That's a valid point, but I don't like the idea of you still trying to pack up your things. You know that, if Silvia finds out that you were fired, it'll make her way too happy, and she'll come looking for you."

"She's already been trying to do that. So now that she's gotten me fired, I don't know what I'm supposed to do," she muttered. "However, I do have two suitcases fully packed. I have a few boxes that I should collapse and put into recycling, and I've got a few bags of toiletries and stuff."

"Can you get them loaded on your own?"

"Yes. I think so. ... I don't know. Look. I'll call you back in a few minutes." And, with that, she disconnected.

"Shit," Burke said, as he stared down at the phone. "I didn't think Silvia would go to her sister's place of work and get her fired."

"It's not something that *normal* people would do," Tiffany noted, "but obviously this sister isn't on the normal side of life."

"No, not right now she isn't. Plus, if she sees that her sister is trying to get away from her, she'll be on the warpath."

"Do you want to go in and help her?"

"Yes, but ... Shirley's right in that, if I'm seen, it will start a full-scale war, and honestly, I would probably be the one fueling the confrontation instead of stopping it. Best case is if we can get Shirley out of there and safely here, without Silvia knowing anything about it."

They were still discussing the pros and cons a few minutes later when Shirley called back. "Okay, I'm already in my car. I just grabbed up everything that I had. I didn't get it cleaned though, so I'll probably lose my deposit."

"Not necessarily, you've still got a few more days left in the month," Burke pointed out in a calm and collected tone. "We could always go back and clean it, if that's what you decide you want to do."

"Oh, right, I guess that's an option."

"Are you driving?"

"I'm just heading out now," she replied. "I know it sounds stupid, but I feel as if time is against me."

"So then move it," Burke stated, "and move it fast because you don't ever ignore those warnings."

"I'm not," she replied, "and I'm already on the way, but it just feels as if they already know or maybe they're coming after me already."

"Then drive," he said urgently, "just drive and get the hell out of the city. If you see them and you can lose them, … do so. Don't get yourself boxed in somewhere. If you can't, don't worry. … Call us. We're here."

"Yeah, you say that, but I don't want to bring them to your doorstep."

"Bring them anyway," Timber stated calmly, his voice a resilient timbre. "We've dealt with those kind of people before."

"You might have, but this one? … Well, he's …"

"I know. He's bad news," Timber confirmed. "So just keep driving."

"And drive fast but safely," Burke added into the phone.

She laughed. "I'm already on the way," she muttered. "God, how did my life come to this? I'll hang up so I can focus on driving."

"You do that," Burke agreed, "and, if you run into trouble, let me know."

"If I run into trouble," she explained, "it'll be coming from them. So, it probably won't be trouble I can get out of easily." And, with that, she disconnected.

"Well, shit," Timber muttered, staring down at Burke's phone. "Is she prone to melodrama?"

"No, not at all. It just shows you how much her sister and that boyfriend terrify her."

"At the moment, it's starting to terrify me too," Timber muttered, staring off in the distance.

Burke got up. "I'll head in her direction and confirm she gets here."

"You do that. I'll get one of the bedrooms set up. If you run into trouble, you know what to do. Don't be a hero, call us, and we'll send reinforcements."

And, with that, Burke grabbed his keys, stepped into his vehicle, and drove down the driveway toward the main road. If nothing else, he would meet her somewhere along the way and could show her where the turnoff was. He also didn't want her followed. It was one thing to bring trouble into the world and have it follow them, but it was another thing entirely to bring an asshole like Silvia's boyfriend into the animal refuge and have to deal with him too.

With that thought firmly in mind, Burke picked up the pace and drove faster.

# CHAPTER 9

S HIRLEY HAD WASTED precious time getting more stuff out of the apartment than she probably needed, but she had this feeling that she needed to grab it now or it wouldn't be there later. Whether her sister would steal it to sell or something else, Shirley didn't know. It made perfect sense to come back later to clean the apartment. Yet she just wasn't looking forward to it, at least not alone. She might get somebody to come with her and stand watch while she cleaned. That way she would get her deposit back, but, if she ended up losing it, so be it.

She drove through town and headed straight out, watching the rearview mirror, looking for anything and everything. When her phone rang, she reached for it and almost clicked on Talk before she realized it was Silvia again.

Her sister left another voice mail message, and Shirley played it while she drove, listening to her sister's furious voice, demanding that Shirley pick up the phone, asking what the hell she was doing and why did she change *their* account. Shirley froze for a moment at that comment. It was *her* account, and Silvia had no rights to it, but that said an awful lot about where her sister's head was at right now, clearly feeling a sense of entitlement.

It was a scary thought, and something Shirley was even more worried about than before. However, she now was also worried about her own safety. Unfortunately, in her sister's case, things had gone too far, and Shirley feared nobody would stop Silvia.

It was horrifying to think that Silvia was so far gone. That account was where Shirley's paychecks went, and she should have taken steps to protect herself a long time ago. It just never occurred to her that Silvia would ever treat Shirley like this. But here it was, her job was gone and her bank account would have been too, if she hadn't moved it.

When the ranting on the phone stopped abruptly, suddenly the voice changed, and the boyfriend spoke. "Where are you?" he asked in a very calm, almost chilling voice. "Not sure what happened between you and your sister, but it needs to be fixed. Call her," he urged. "You don't want us to come after you."

He left it at that, but to hear him say it, and say it the way he did, made the hackles on the back of Shirley's neck rise, and she realized just how terrified she was of him. Silvia didn't seem to have any problem with him, but, for Shirley, he was someone to be avoided.

She had followed Timber's directions as best she could, but she was rattled and worried she might not find where she was going. She kept on driving, going blindly now. Just when she thought she might be coming up to the target road sign, she slowed down, and there in front of her was a vehicle parked. Her heart skipped a beat for a moment, until she realized it was Burke. She slowed down and pulled onto the side of the road, right up beside him.

He rolled down his window and smiled at her. "Any problems?" he asked.

She shook her head. "No, not really." At that, his eyebrows popped up, as if he didn't believe her, and she shrugged. "Silvia left me a message, and honestly, it scared me because she seems to have convinced herself that it was her bank account."

"What do you mean?"

"She was giving me shit for having taken the money out of the bank account, closing *our* account as she called it," she explained.

"But it's your account?"

"Yes, … it's my account. Mine and mine alone. It's my name on it, and my paychecks went into it. She never ever contributed."

"Did you ever say that it was her money too?"

"No, … never. And it wasn't as if I gave her my cards either. She took them and then wouldn't give them back. I didn't really care about it back then," she added, "but now is a very different story. At the time those credit cards were more of an emergency fund for me. However, now I know more about her, and she's more likely to take advantage of my savings account now," she explained.

"That's crazy, and now you've lost your job because of her."

"Yeah, that wasn't fun."

"I'm sorry. That's not what anybody wants to have happen."

"No, and I still can't believe it. Silvia is a whole different story. And her boyfriend left me a chilling message too."

"Play it for me and Timber when we get there. For now, just follow me."

"I'm so glad you are here. I was afraid I was lost," she shared. "Honestly, I spent the whole time looking behind me, and now I'm still feeling … tense and stressed."

"Both of those reactions are totally understandable," he

agreed, with a nod. "Let's get you up to Timber's place and out of the public eye."

"Right." She frowned. "That's a really good point." She followed Burke down the road a bit, when he pulled into an open yard where multiple vehicles were parked. Something about seeing that many vehicles around made her feel so much safer. She parked beside one, pulling up right next to Burke.

He got out and asked her, "Is there any reason to think they might be tracking you?"

She frowned at him. "Tracking me? Oh, good God," she muttered. "I have no idea, but Frankie is …"

"Frankie is what?"

She stopped. "Scary."

He nodded and looked over to where Timber sat on the front porch. He got up, went inside, and then came back out again with some tool in his hand. He quickly scanned Shirley's vehicle and announced, "The vehicle is clear."

"Thank heavens for that," she muttered, relieved. "You just opened up a fear I hadn't even considered."

He nodded and smiled at her. "I'm Timber."

"Glad to finally put a face to the name and to the voice," she replied. "I'm Shirley, sister of the con artist, apparently."

Burke clarified, "Actually that would be daughter of the con artist, sister of the fraud machine."

She winced and nodded. "Yeah, and apparently now she's upset that I took away *our* money."

"Explain," Timber ordered, his voice hard.

And Shirley did. "My sister has deluded herself into believing that the bank account was somehow suddenly *ours*. She was furious that I had moved *our* money."

"And was it?"

"No," she declared. "It's all mine. She took my bank cards a while back, and I told her there was no point in using them because no money was there," she added.

"Did she ever make withdrawals?"

"When she took the cards, I had just started my job and didn't have any money in that account for a while. The real money that I have is invested, and I didn't think she knew about that or could access those funds, all saved from my earlier job, where I made some good money. However, recently I've been working as a receptionist for a while and living pretty frugally, until she now cost me that job. Yet it didn't even occur to me that she would try to cash out my investment money, not until this all blew up. So I moved it all, right before I saw her show up at that bank, trying to get some cash."

"Of course she did. If Burke's credit card scams weren't working, they needed another mark," Timber noted, frowning at her, "and this time it was you."

She nodded. "I canceled my cards yesterday," she shared, "and I've got new ones coming, but, of course, that will be through the mail." Then she frowned.

"You need to contact them and find out if they've already been sent out," Burke suggested.

"Where were they going?" Timber asked.

"To my home address," she replied, frowning as she thought about it. "That's probably not where I want them to land, is it?"

"No, because she can check your mail, I presume?"

"Yes, and she will. She also told me that she had keys made to my apartment."

"She told you all this?" Burke asked.

"Yeah, she thought it was a big lark," Shirley explained.

"Now, of course, I'm seeing it in a very different light, and it's not a big lark at all, and I'll be at the receiving end of her cons."

"Particularly if she causes any damage to the apartment," Timber pointed out, standing at her side.

"Did you contact the landlord?" Burke asked.

"No," she said. "I didn't have a chance to clean it or anything. I just grabbed my stuff and ran."

"But if she has keys, is she likely to go in there and find out that you've skipped out on her?" Burke asked, sharing a look with Timber.

"Yes," she confirmed, scrubbing her face.

"Do you have your landlord's number?" Timber asked. She gave it to Timber, who nodded and asked, "Would you mind if I spoke to him?"

"Not at all. I don't even know what to do with the whole situation."

"No need to worry. I'll call him and see if he can intercept those bank cards at the very least." With that, he headed inside.

She looked over at Burke. "He really is helpful, isn't he?"

"Yeah, he's the best," Burke confirmed, with a smile. "I came here, and I just needed a place to land for a couple of days, and Timber gave it to me. And here I am, even a several weeks later."

She turned and looked around. "Is everybody here for the same reason?"

He laughed. "No. Some are here because they are friends of friends. Some are recovering from God-only-knows-what. Many of them are people who work with Kat and Badger, who are military friends to all of us," he shared. "Kat was the designer who I told you about."

"Right." Shirley nodded. "The woman who does all the prosthetics."

"Yes," he replied, with a smile. "She and Badger have an awful big crew of mostly veterans, who they support in any number of ways. They've been building houses for other veterans, or just renovating them to accommodate their injuries. So, from Kat and Badger's perspective, Timber's place is just another house, just another friend who needs a hand."

"But it's a huge hand," Shirley noted, as she stared at all the buildings. "My God, he's got … so much space here."

"And that's what he needs for his animal refuge," he noted. "Oh, and, just so you know, there's a squirrel here named Dodger, and an owl named Gibraltar," he shared, as she watched all around her, her mouth open. "A bobcat slinks in and around the place. He's called Billy Bob. Just don't make sudden movements around him or the bear that comes around sometimes. No need to be alarmed if you see either of them. Big Mike may be a bear, but he has been harmless so far, even to the other injured animals we have here."

She frowned at him and asked, "You're joking, right?"

"No, … I'm not. Timber is some kind of animal whisperer and healer, so they gravitate to him when they need help. We also have an armadillo here at times too. I don't know his name. He tends to be really quiet or not-so-friendly to newcomers."

She just stared at him and shook her head. "I had no idea."

"And some rescue horses just arrived, to add to the few other horses and the donkey that were already here. … The donkey would be Danny. I'm not sure I even know how many dogs are here right now," he said, with a laugh. "When we sat outside having coffee this morning, we had Big Mike wandering the yard."

She just stared at him in shocked delight.

He laughed. "You don't seem to be upset about it."

"No, are you kidding?" She laughed. "That's fabulous, and I can't think of anything nicer."

Just then Timber returned and joined them outside. "So, I just talked to your landlord and explained the situation. He'll cancel the lease right now, and he's changing the locks. His buddy is on his way over right now to take care of that. He'll watch your mail and set it aside for one of us to pick up later."

"Did you get everything out?" Burke asked her.

She nodded. "I got 99 percent of it anyway. If I left anything, I'll have to apologize to him. I just couldn't get out fast enough."

"And he understands that now," Timber told her. "He is someone we've dealt with before, which helped." When she stared at Timber in shock, he just nodded. "In this industry it's all about who you know. Anyway he's got the locksmith coming, but you probably will lose your deposit."

"That's fine," she muttered, "considering he's having to change the locks and that he's letting me off the hook on cleaning it and the rest of it, I'm fine with that."

Timber nodded and added, "He doesn't know whether anybody has been there looking for you or not, but there have been a couple complaints from the neighbors about noise."

She winced at that. "And, of course, that'll be Silvia, right?"

"It's hard to say. Yet, once the locks have been changed,

he'll post a notice that the apartment is for rent, so your sister will know you're no longer there."

"I don't know what she and Frankie will do when they see that." She sighed. "It could really send her off the deep end."

Timber tilted his head. "That may be, but it also could be exactly the wake-up call your sister needs."

"Sure, but now that she feels entitled to my money and to my home, and intentionally caused such drama that I lost my job, I don't know what I'm supposed to do," she shared, sadness in her gaze.

"What do you want to do? Do you want to contact her and let her know where you are?" Timber asked.

"God no," she muttered.

"And is that because of her, or because of her boyfriend?"

She stared at him for a long moment, then reluctantly replied, "Both."

"Good. Keep that in mind. Your sister is no longer the same person she was. She's become someone who is very free with other people's money and belongings," Timber acknowledged. "That isn't a person anybody needs in their world. We are good hard-working citizens, and the last thing we want around here is anybody who'll just take whatever they want and not give a crap."

"I hear you," she said. "Are you sure I can stay here? I might be bringing trouble to your doorstep."

"Absolutely you are welcome here," Timber declared, with a smile. "And listen. Even if Silvia does find you here, remember that you're not alone. Some people will always be around here at any time of day or night. Oh, and that's not all. You'll need to keep an eye out for some wildlife around here."

"I already heard about a few of the animals, even some with names," she replied, with a big smile. "If I can help with any of them, let me know."

"What skills do you have?"

She winced. "My training and certification is in project management, so not exactly what you need. Other than that, most recently I was working as a receptionist." She laughed. "Again, not something you need."

"On the other hand," Burke noted, turning to her, "didn't you work at animal rescues at one time?"

"Sure, I did," she confirmed. "I did work with a shelter for several years. I was horse crazy back then, but I also worked with a lot of reptiles."

"Reptiles?" Timber asked, his eyebrows shooting up.

She nodded. "One of the few women who didn't mind working with a snake," she replied, with a smile.

"I don't have any snakes right now," he noted, "but, if you want to work with any of animals, there's lots of work to be done."

"Absolutely," she declared. "When you're working with animals, it's not really work."

"Exactly," he agreed, with a smile. He turned to Burke. "I like her."

Just then Dwight yelled from the front porch, "Get your butts inside. It's dinnertime."

# CHAPTER 10

BURKE WOKE UP the next morning, bright and early, and headed downstairs. He stopped outside her room, but it was quiet. With a smile, he hoped that she'd managed to get some sleep after all the chaos she had gone through yesterday. He went into the kitchen to find some coffee. He stopped in surprise, when there she was, sitting comfortably, talking to Toby and Dwight.

She looked up and smiled at him. "Hey."

"Hey, yourself. Did you get any sleep?" he asked in concern. "I stopped by your door to check on you, but there wasn't a sound, so I assumed you were sleeping."

She shrugged. "I slept fine, and then all of a sudden I wasn't sleeping fine." She gave half a laugh. "I was awake and not likely to go back to sleep again, so, once I heard some movement down here, I got up. I didn't want to disturb anybody," she said, then frowned at Burke. "Did I wake you?"

"Nope, not at all," he replied, "and, even if you did, it would be fine."

She smiled. "I'd forgotten how easy you are to get along with."

He frowned at her. "Somehow that didn't seem to come across as a compliment."

She laughed. "Probably because I wasn't trying to give

you a compliment. I literally just remembered how easy you were to get along with," she stated, with a shrug, "but you can take it any way you want to."

"I'll take it," he conceded, with a mocking smile. "Don't worry about that." He walked over, poured himself a cup of coffee, then glanced over at Toby and Dwight, both studiously ignoring them. "Did we interrupt your breakfast or your quiet time?"

Toby shrugged. "If it wasn't you guys, it would be somebody else soon enough," he noted, with a yawn and a stretch. Two dogs at his feet got up and stretched too.

She chuckled. "I absolutely love how they mimic everybody else in this world."

Toby nodded, then looked down at the stretching dogs and smiled. "These two are Kojack and Philly. The little basset hound is called Little Toby, and he's mine."

"Besides, they can mimic me anytime they want," Dwight suggested, with a gentle grin on his face. "They are awesome company."

"They are indeed," she agreed. "And the two King Charles spaniels in the basket?" She pointed out the dog bed at one side. "You're very blessed to have them. What are their names?"

"That's Lucy and Bing."

Dwight stood up. "In this business, some people just don't seem to understand how important breakfast is."

"I most definitely understand how important breakfast is." She hopped to her feet and asked, "Can I help you?"

He frowned at her and shook her head. "Not today, ... no."

She looked back over at Burke, who just laughed and added, "And he means it. However, even if it's a no today, it might be a yes tomorrow."

"What's the difference?" she asked in confusion.

Burke shrugged. "Depends on what he's cooking, what his plan is," he shared, with a smile. "So don't worry about it. If he said no, he meant no, and it doesn't mean anything more than that."

She nodded but wasn't exactly sure if she was supposed to do something anyway. So, when Burke got up and started to clear off the table, she jumped in to help. By the time they had the table set, she realized just how many men were here. "Do they all come in at once?"

"No, they sure don't. Any number of men may come and go throughout brunch. Some eat breakfast. Some don't. Some say they won't but show up and eat anyway. It's just life."

She wasn't sure how that was life—certainly not hers to date—but she was just trying to not rock the boat and to make herself useful. She appreciated having a place to come to, yet she knew it was temporary, and she didn't want to overstay her welcome. But how was she to not overstay her welcome when she didn't even know how long the welcome was good for? Or how it was supposed to work here?

As she sat back down again, she looked around at Burke and then Toby. "Is there more I should be doing?" she asked in a low voice.

Burke smiled at her. "No, you're fine."

"Are you sure? I really appreciate the fact that I had this place to come to," she shared, "because God only knows what yesterday was all about."

"That's why I'm surprised you slept at all."

"Honestly, I think it was just the relief of being safe. I know that sounds terrible, but ..."

"No, it sounds perfectly normal," Dwight noted, from beside the stove. "Nothing quite like that safety to make you suddenly realize that you're exhausted and that you can finally let go and just relax for a few minutes," he shared. "And you don't have to do anything here. You're welcome to be here, and we'll do everything we can to keep you safe while you're here."

Toby frowned at her. "I can already see how that somehow bothers you."

"It's," she began cautiously, "just definitely not something I'm used to."

He snorted. "I hear you there, but that doesn't mean a whole lot in this day and age because, when you need help, you need help, and there's just nothing else for it."

"Go grab the eggs out of the fridge, will you?" Dwight asked her.

She walked over to the fridge, opened it up, and noted it was stocked full of breakfast foods. "I presume you have a second fridge somewhere," she noted, as she grabbed a couple dozen and brought them over to him.

He looked at her and nodded. "Go grab another dozen."

Her eyebrows shot up, and she headed back over and picked up a third dozen. "So, they're all big eaters?"

"Every one of them," he declared, with a smile. "And I would rather they were big eaters than noneaters."

"Oh, I'm right there with you," she agreed. "I just really didn't expect you to go through that many eggs."

"Oh, this is nothing," he replied, "but, right now, we'll do pancakes. You know how to flip pancakes?"

"I do." Using the batter he'd already made up, she quickly started cooking flapjacks on the griddle. By the time she had twenty or so off to one side in a lidded warming tray, she noted that a few of the men had come in already.

She had said hi to a couple but now realized others were here too. She knew there would be questions, since she had come in last night, had been here for dinner, but had also stayed overnight. That in itself was something that most people would be curious about, but thankfully nobody mentioned anything over breakfast. She continued to flip flapjacks as long as there was batter, and, when she was done, she washed up the containers.

Dwight pointed at the table. "Go sit."

She laughed. "I guess you give orders all the time, *huh*?"

He nodded. "Pretty much." Then he grinned at her. "And it's better if I bark orders at you, instead of you getting into trouble over something that could have been fixed because you didn't listen to a bark."

"Oh, I'm pretty good at listening to orders," she shared, "and, back in my project management days, I barked a few myself."

He laughed, and she just smiled, took a seat, and polished off a decent-size breakfast herself. When Timber showed up, instead of coming from upstairs, he came in from outside.

She looked over at Burke. "*Uh-oh*, should we have gotten up earlier?"

He shook his head. "No, we're fine." Then he looked back at Timber. "Any news?"

He shook his head. "It's all quiet."

"That's good," Burke said, with a yawn. He stood up, throwing back the last of his coffee, and said, "I'll start in the barns, working with the horses."

"You have horses?" she asked.

"Seems you forgot in all the chaos, but we've got some

rescue horses that came in, plus Sparky, who has been with Timber for a long time."

"And a donkey too. I heard him early this morning."

"That's Danny," Toby pointed out. "He is older and had been abused, but he's doing just fine now. We got him after some jackass hurt him, and he ran in here, wounds all over his belly." He exchanged a glance with Timber.

Burke noted the shared look, wondering what that was all about. He added, "Danny's kicking up a bit of a fuss over the newest arrivals, the additional horses."

"In what way?" she asked, as she got up and helped to clear off the table.

"He wants to join them, to say hi, but we've kept him separated for now, and have some of the horses separated from each other as well. We've also got some farrier work to do today."

She nodded. "Are you okay if I give you a hand out there?"

"That would be great. There are always stalls to muck out," he teased.

She groaned. "Should have seen that coming, but I've got no problem doing that either." And, with that, the two of them headed off.

As she got out to the barn, alone with Burke now, she whispered, "I feel a little uncomfortable around the men."

He frowned at her. "Uncomfortable being around the men, or uncomfortable because of the men?"

"Not because of the men," she clarified. "I just want to help where I can, but I don't want to get in the way."

"Ah," he muttered, "and that's a different thing altogether."

"Maybe. I don't want to split hairs about it. I just want

to fit in."

He laid a hand on her shoulder. "You just got here last night and don't even know your way around the place yet. Try to relax a bit and give yourself a chance to settle in."

She sighed. "I suppose so. I'm really not trying to be difficult."

He faced her and stated, "You need to let go of everything concerning that family of yours. Fitting in isn't something that you have to do. It's not a requirement. Getting along is a requirement," he noted, with a laugh, "but trying to fit into a place with all the moving parts this one has is a pretty tall order."

"I really appreciate the fact that I was able to get here, safe and sound. I know I need to be figuring out where I'm going from here, but—"

Immediately he placed a finger against her lips. "That's not the issue for this moment."

She took a deep breath and let it out slowly. "Do you think I can stay here for a couple days?" she asked anxiously. "Or do I need to leave today?"

He looked at her in surprise. "Oh, wow. Okay." He stepped back. "I didn't realize that was already worrying you."

"Of course it is," she replied. "I don't have the slightest idea where I should go, but a part of me says I need to go to a completely different state."

"Where would you want to go?"

"I don't know," she admitted. "I prefer California, with the weather and the water and the palm trees, except I don't really like people."

He burst out laughing at that. "I'm not in favor of California for you, especially if you don't like people," he quipped. "New York might be a better choice, if you don't like people, as I hear they never say hi to anybody."

She giggled at that. "It's such a well-known saying that you wonder if it's even true," she shared, with a laugh.

"I don't know," he admitted, "but I would just as soon have nobody talk to me. California is out for me," he declared. "I don't think I would want to live with that many people."

"I was thinking about that too," she replied, "but I want some space. I have some money set aside," she confessed. "At least I do right now, … thanks to you. I was just at the point of taking a chunk of my receptionist paycheck and putting it into investments again. Since I lost that job, I don't have anything to invest right now. Thank God Silvia didn't get to that investment fund. If I'd lost it, it would have been a blow."

"Of course, and let's not even think about any of that right now," he suggested. "We'll deal with some of that later, and I'm sure there will be phone calls and God-only-knows what else."

"Yeah, my sister isn't one to give up easily," Shirley noted, "even more so with her boyfriend egging her on."

"After hearing his voice mail message to you, you definitely need to stay *no contact* with them."

"Sure, I need to, but that doesn't mean it will be all that easy."

"As long as you're here, and you don't go to town, it should be fine," he pointed out. "In town is where she would most likely find you."

"I know, but now that my apartment and my job are out of the picture," she mentioned, with a note of bitterness, "I don't know where she would expect to find me or would even begin to look for me."

"Maybe she wouldn't expect to find you anywhere. Maybe she thought that you would turn to her."

"Oh, God no," she muttered. "No way anybody would ever turn to her. She can't even begin to look after herself."

"She's doing just fine," he pointed out, "not in a legally or morally ethical way, but—"

"That doesn't matter to her one bit," Shirley declared, with a headshake. "And you're right. I can't make any decisions or judgments about her at this point. She's made enough bad decisions, and I just have to live with it."

"We always have to live with it when dealing with someone like that," he clarified. "You can try talking with them until you are blue in the face, but, if they choose to continue on that same path, there is nothing else to be done."

She smiled. "Let's get on with the day, and maybe, if I get lots of hard work in, I'll completely forget about her."

And that's what they did. They had mucked out the stalls, and he checked up on the hooves of the couple horses he'd worked with. Then they'd been given the vitamins and extra supplements mixed into the feed for the one mare. Burke and Shirley were deep in the zone by this time. He trimmed more hooves, then led those two horses outside to join the others.

A lot of welcoming neighs came from the horses on the other side of the fence, and then she saw the donkey was here as well. She walked over to him, curry brush in hand, and he nickered softly, which was an interesting response because normally they would bray fairly loudly. Just as she was about to step back, he started to bray, as if to stop her. She laughed and got closer and began brushing him. This went on for a bit, until she realized he literally was keeping her there.

Finally she had to step back. "Sorry, baby, but I can't stay here with you all the time, as other animals need attention too."

He nudged her several more times, then realizing that his turn was up, he walked away from her, heading toward the other horses.

Burke joined her soon afterward. "I see that Danny likes you."

"He likes the attention, and he definitely likes being brushed," she shared, with a smile for him. "At some point in time Danny must have been well loved."

"Yes, he was. Then the lady of the house passed on, and her husband didn't quite know what to do with Danny but kept him. However, Danny got no attention. Then his grandson decided that the donkey should be the target for his frustrations with life." When she turned and glared at him, he shrugged. "Remember that most of the animals here have horrible backstories, at least for a part of their lives."

She winced and nodded. "That's the nature of rescue work, but I don't want to focus on that," she muttered. "Yet we can never forget, can we?"

"No, we can't," he agreed, "nor should we."

She grimaced. "You're right."

Just as they were about to break for lunch, or at least she hoped so because she was suddenly feeling incredibly hungry, her phone rang. She reached for it automatically, then froze.

He looked over at her and nodded. "Good response."

She winced and when a message was left, she played it, and of course it was Silvia again—angry and sounding well beyond furious.

"Answer the damn phone, will you?"

Then she found several other voice mails she hadn't listened to. As she continued to play through them, her sister's tone went from being angry to *Starting to get worried* to *Come on, sis. Don't do this* to *At least let me know you're alive.* Shirley was shaking when she shut off the messages and looked over at him.

He stared at her in concern.

"It's just so hard," she whispered.

"I understand. I know it's hard, but in this case to protect yourself …"

She nodded. "*No contact*," she repeated, "but wow. … That won't be easy." She took several slow, deep breaths.

"Do you think she's actually worried about you?"

She shrugged. "She's probably worried in the sense that the money just isn't available to her anymore." Then she winced. "Wow, do I sound bitter and angry at the whole world?"

"And that's all right too," he replied. "You're seeing the other side of your family."

"I've known about this side. It's just … I guess I've always managed to look past it because it wasn't directed at me."

"But not now."

"No, not now," she confirmed, her tone determined. When the phone rang yet again a few minutes later, she winced.

"You can turn off the ringer, you know?" Burke suggested.

"I could," she agreed, with a laugh, "but I guess I left it on thinking there might be phone calls from somebody else." Then she gave a self-deprecating laugh. "Which would mean that I have friends, and the truth of the matter is, I don't know anybody else who would be calling me." Taking a deep breath, she shut off the ringer and muttered, "God, what a sad awakening."

"But it is an awakening, and you can't do anything about it, until you recognize what the problem is."

She looked over at him and quipped, "What problem? I have no friends, and I have to start fresh, as in completely all over again. I thought I was doing that by taking the receptionist job and by living in that small apartment. I made a legitimate effort to settle in. I'd sold what was left in my prior apartment, after the supposed theft and after leaving the project management position."

"Do you want to go back to that?"

"No way," she replied instantly. "If there was ever a job guaranteed to put you in a hospital and to score you a heart attack, that's the one," she muttered. "Angry people all the time, job schedules that you can't work with, timelines that aren't reasonable. So tight that you can't even begin to function, and, no matter what you say or do, it never changes. And, because you can't ever maintain, I always felt like the weak link at every meeting," she admitted.

"Nobody ever seemed to point it out, but it was always there, clearly obvious who had the lowest success at making the deadlines," she shared. "And yet I wasn't making those deadlines. I was trying to make other people make those deadlines. It always seemed to be my team's failure to cooperate, so management would say that it was up to me to make them comply, but ..." She gave a half laugh. "Either I am not miserable enough to force other people to do the ridiculous shit they didn't want to do," she explained, "or I just was too kind and not pounding on them hard enough. I don't know. The job definitely wasn't what I thought it would be, and it wasn't for me. I really enjoyed the work I did in school, but I had no idea what the real world application would be like. I just didn't feel right passing along impossible deadlines, putting the poor planning label on the backs of my employees and their families, so I didn't."

"So that job in particular was bad," he pointed out, "but that doesn't mean every job will be like that."

"No, maybe not, but … it was definitely an eye-opener into my personality and into what I want out of life. Sometimes you have to see what you don't like to help define what you do," she noted, with a smile.

"Of course."

As they walked back to the kitchen, she said, "I can see why Dwight took over the kitchen."

He looked at her and asked, "And why is that?"

"Because you're not dealing with other people. … He puts a meal on the table, and they either eat it or they don't," she explained. "I kind of like that."

"And yet I can envision that you would be plagued with doubts, worried that everybody didn't like it, and that you should have cooked something else."

She frowned, then burst out laughing. "Unfortunately that is very true."

"And that's because you care."

"Yeah, but that doesn't mean that Dwight doesn't care," she clarified, as she stepped into the main house. At that, several of the men turned and looked at her, and she flushed. "I was just …"

Dwight looked at her and interjected, "I do care, though I'm not sure what that conversation was about. Sometimes I think I care too much."

She gave him a big smile, then walked over and, on impulse, hugged the older man. "I was talking about the problems that come with being a project manager, and the stress that was involved in trying to push people to do things they either weren't capable of doing because the deadlines were impossibly tight, or when they had no intention of listening to me because of personality conflicts or God-only-knows what," she explained, raising her hands. "So, I used you as an example, saying that your work here in this kitchen is nice in a way because you put a meal on the table and people either eat it or they don't."

Burke continued that recap. "And that's when I stepped in to say that it wouldn't be like that for her because she would still be worried that she'd cooked the wrong thing or that she should have done better."

Toby smiled. "And you're both right," he noted. "It is nice to have a job where you can just do something and step back with the attitude that, if somebody doesn't like it, it's too damn bad. However, like Shirley, if people didn't like it, I would feel the need to change the menu so people would want to eat more."

"And then I would step in and tell him not to because the last freaking thing we need around here is people eating more," Timber declared with a huge grin, obviously joking.

The men started laughing, razzing him about worrying about his bottom line.

Timber nodded. "And, of course, I'm kidding because I really want everybody here to eat well so you can keep working." That set off a new round of laughter, the camaraderie here evident.

Impulsively Shirley looked over at him and asked, "Do you keep any schedules or timelines? Do you have any idea of what all needs to be done and in what order?" When he tapped his noggin, she shook her head. "And that's a good way to get messed up."

"Oh, no doubt. It is a good way to get messed up," he agreed, "and I've already done it many times, but I don't really know how to keep it organized." Then he frowned at her. "Unless you want to take that on."

She frowned right back at him and said, "You might not like what I tell you."

He laughed. "In that case, I won't have any trouble telling you to butt out and to stay in your lane."

She winced. "And I might take that in the wrong way, and you'll send me to my vehicle in tears."

"So, we would have to find a way to get along and to communicate better," Timber suggested.

"I wasn't planning on telling you how to do anything," she clarified, with a chuckle. "It's more a case of trying to keep you organized as to what you need to do, and making sure you know the potential impacts of decisions to do things differently than planned."

"Keeping me organized would save us from having to go back and fix things that were backassward."

"Especially seeing how we forgot a bunch of things that needed to happen on the bunkhouse," one of the men pointed out. "Even to just have a single written list of everything that needs to be done, where we could see it, would be helpful. Some of us are better equipped to work on some projects than others, so that would be helpful in terms of deciding who should be working on what."

Timber nodded at him. "That is something we've talked about, isn't it?"

"It sure is, and, if you had somebody who could help get you organized and could put in a system you would maintain going forward, it could really be a good thing."

"A system *I* can maintain? You guys seem to think I can't maintain anything," he noted suspiciously, glaring at them. But his lips were twitching. He looked over at her and asked, "How did you do at the barn?"

"It was great. I absolutely loved it."

He nodded. "There is something gloriously good for all of us about reaching out and helping animals, isn't there?"

"Reaching out and helping animals, plus doing some physical work for the first time in a while, was helpful. Just being able to do something constructive with a tangible result is good, uplifting even."

"Which is why we need you to help organize it," the same burly man added, with a laugh.

Timber sighed. "I think what they're trying to say is, it might help us all be more effective if you could get me organized. Initially I didn't think I *wasn't* organized," he shared, glaring at the men. "But there has been a couple times lately where we've got the cart before the horse and missed some of the things that needed to be done."

Shirley nodded. "Even a project board with a long to-do list would be a better system than having it all in your head."

"I have a massive to-do list," he agreed, "but, yeah, it would be helpful if others could see it."

"Do you have any whiteboards? Or a chalkboard? Anything like that?" she asked.

He looked at her with one eyebrow raised and asked, "Do I look like I have anything like that?"

She laughed. "No, not really," she replied, with a smile. "But I can do it with big sheets of paper for now, like brown paper used for padding shipping boxes. For so many people we don't really want it to be down on something small, like printer paper," she explained. "You can certainly do that if you have finite schedules, but, if you're talking about some big overarching project, it would really help to have big paper to work from."

He just frowned at her.

"And I suspect there's really no money for that either, is there?" She looked around, trying to think of what she could use to set up master schedules. "I can use printer paper and just tape them all together," she offered.

"That would probably take a lot more work than just getting a couple whiteboards," Timber replied, as he brought up his phone and started checking something out. "Is that what you're looking for?" He brought his phone to her.

She looked down at it and smiled. "Two of those would be really helpful."

"They're pretty big," he told her.

She looked around, pointed up to the one big wall in the dining area. "While you're doing so much charting and building, that would be the place for it. Everybody could come in and could see the work that needs to be done, what's on top, what needs to be started next, then go from there."

When he remained a little doubtful, she smiled and added, "And we don't have to do any of it."

He looked over at her. "You say that now, but *they* won't say that."

"Maybe not," she noted, with a shrug. "But it's your place and your system, so whatever works best for you is what we'll do."

"And yet," he added, "it needs to be what works best for everyone here. We have a lot of small jobs that we're all individually trying to keep track of as well, but we don't have one central place for noting all of them."

"Good," she stated, as she looked down at the cost of the whiteboards and shrugged. "Order them, and I'll pay for them. I'm not doing anything, and I'm hardly contributing."

He snorted at that. "You're not paying for some whiteboards to help get me organized," he muttered, and he quickly sent through the order. "Next person who goes to town can pick them up."

"Good enough," she said, with a smile. "And what would that look like?"

He turned to her and frowned. "Will you be this pushy when you want to get that list going?"

She gave him a broad grin. "I will be a lot pushier when I want to get that list going because somehow I'll have to get it out of your brain, so other people can work on it."

He sighed, looked over at Toby and Dwight, caught them both grinning from ear to ear. "What are you smirking about? Wait until she wants to revamp your kitchen and the menu."

The smile immediately fell off Dwight's face as he stood up and declared, "She can stay out of my damn kitchen."

Shirley grinned. "Gee, and here I thought maybe cinnamon buns or something like that would be a good thing for today."

Toby was about to repeat Dwight's warning, but he stopped. "Wait. What? … You bake?"

She nodded. "I can bake. I'm not good at putting together anything more than basic meals for myself, and I'm not good at having things all cooked and ready to eat at the same time like you are," she admitted, with a shrug, "but I can bake."

"Cinnamon buns?" one of the men repeated.

She nodded. "Cinnamon buns. Great big pans full of them."

The man looked over at Timber. "If she can bake cinnamon buns too, the cost of those whiteboards is nothing." And with, that he turned and walked away.

She looked over at Burke, who was grinning madly. "Does that mean cinnamon buns are a yes or a no?" she asked cautiously.

"It means yes," Burke replied, "particularly if the rest of us have any say in the matter."

"I figured that was a given," she replied, with a laugh. "I've never known men to *not* want their sweets."

"It's one thing to have the sweets," he clarified, with a chuckle, "but cinnamon buns are always a fan favorite."

She smiled. "Good to know." And, with that, she looked over at Timber. "Are you okay if I step into the kitchen and make some stuff?"

He stared at her in surprise. "I don't mind at all, and Dwight and Toby have already given you the okay," he noted. "So I'm just clarifying that fact that you said *cinnamon buns*, so an awful lot of men will be looking for those today."

She laughed. "That's fine. I have no whiteboard to work on, so I can bake." And she walked toward the kitchen.

Burke asked, "Do you need a recipe?"

She looked back at him, shook her head, and said, "Nope, I sure don't. This is my grandmother's recipe, and I've been making it for years."

And, with a bright smile on her face, she stepped into the kitchen and joined Toby and Dwight.

# CHAPTER 11

BURKE WATCHED AS Shirley spoke to Dwight for a minute, after he pointed out where she could find what she needed, and she then set to work.

Timber turned to Burke and asked, "Does she bake?"

"Dang if I know. Silvia couldn't boil water—or flat-out refused."

He burst out laughing. "It sounds as if you were barking up the wrong tree before."

"That's for sure," he declared, with feeling. "Shirley was really good in the barn today, great with the animals, happy to muck out the stalls, not a wimp and not a whiner. She got right to work. You know, down the road," he added for emphasis, "when you have some time to focus on operational details instead of construction, some equipment might be a nice addition."

"Yeah, I've got some equipment coming," Timber confirmed. "It's just a matter of timing. I'm talking to Andy about some of what he's got over there."

"Oh, that makes perfect sense. He's probably got exactly what you need already."

"He does, but that doesn't mean he's necessarily ready to part with it all."

"Of course not." Burke snorted. "Parting with it probably means the end of an era for him."

"In a way it is the end of an era, whether he's quite ready for it or not, but it's easy enough to understand why he wouldn't be quite ready to see it all come to end so soon."

Leaving Shirley in the kitchen with Toby, Burke headed outside with Timber. "The horses are doing fine. Everybody is out and looking okay, so what's next?"

"Either working on construction or taking a look at that well, I guess." He shook his head and raised both hands. "She's right. I really need to have it all written down someplace so we can keep better track of it."

"In fairness, your system probably wasn't so bad when you were doing it all yourself—up until you suddenly ended up with a full crew without even asking for them," he pointed out. "Now that you have all these people, it makes more sense to get organized so you can make the most efficient use of them. She's right about that."

He sighed. "I do have to go into town and get supplies, so maybe I'll run by and get the whiteboards myself. I'll also go talk to the bank."

"Money problems?" Burke asked, turning to face him.

"Nope, I saved up quite a bit. Plus, I inherited some," Timber shared. "So money isn't the issue, but I might need to open up a few investments and unlock some of that."

"Any trouble?"

"The trouble with doing that is," he pointed out, "as soon as you start spending principal ..." He let his voice trail off because Burke understood as well as Timber did.

"I know," Burke confirmed, "but what else would you do when you went from a one-man operation to suddenly having all that help, accelerating the project well beyond what you ever imagined? You had no choice but to confirm they had everything they needed."

Just then they heard a vehicle coming down the road. As he watched the truck approach, Timber had a big smile on his face, as he walked over and talked to the other man. Burke stayed on the sidelines, close but not quite, until he was officially introduced to Andy Killerman, the man who had sold Timber this land.

He smiled at the older man and greeted him. Andy nodded at him, then looked back at Timber. "You've really got quite a crew here, don't you?"

"It wasn't planned," Timber clarified, "but when men show up …"

Andy nodded. "When the labor is there, you've got to put it to good use." He looked around. "I guess it's probably time we talked about some of that equipment, isn't it?"

Timber nodded. "It is, though I've also got to keep my budget in mind."

"I understand that. I really do. As soon as we settled up on the property, I figured you would eventually need the equipment."

"I do," he admitted, with a laugh, "but this whole project has accelerated really quickly, with all the help I've gotten, so my budget has been turned upside down. I've got options. Still, I need to keep my bottom line and cash flow in mind."

"Of course, everything's got a bottom line, doesn't it?" Andy agreed, with a sigh. "Anyway, I won't be needing this equipment anymore, so I thought maybe I could make a real good deal for you."

Timber nodded. "That would be great, but your idea of a *real good deal* and mine might be different. What equipment are we talking about?"

"I've got a front-end loader, a tractor, a couple flatbed

trailers and, of course, horse trailers. You'll probably need almost everything," he noted, as he looked around. He smiled when he saw the horses out in the pasture. "What? You've already got more out there?" he exclaimed. "That's a sight."

"We had those come in yesterday, and of course I already had yours here."

"Right."

When Danny started to bray in his direction, Andy walked over to the fence, and the donkey came flying. The two old friends greeted each other, and he smiled as he looked back at Timber. "It's good to see him doing so well."

"It is. He'll be just fine here, Andy."

"I can see that," he agreed. "I guess I should have done this a long time ago."

"But if you had, he wouldn't be here with me now, would he?" Timber pointed out, with a bright smile. "He's happy, and he's got quite a load of friends here. Speaking of which, we haven't spoken about your other horses either."

"I know."

"What do you want to do?" Timber asked Andy.

"I've sold four of them," he shared, with a nod. "I've got three older ones that just need a place to live. … So, for their care, I was thinking about trading you some of the equipment." He turned to look at Timber.

Timber stared at Andy. "You want to exchange for the horses' care?"

"The horses are my responsibility, but honestly, I'm not sure I can care for them much longer. I could sell them off for meat, but that won't suit me. Plus, I can feel my wife shivering with anger at the very thought," he muttered. "So, yeah, I was thinking maybe we should go to my place and take a look and see what you can use, and maybe we can come to a deal then."

With that, Timber nodded. "Sounds great to me. Let's go."

And, with that, the two men hopped into Andy's old truck, and they headed back down to his place.

Burke stayed at the open doorway to the main cabin and watched as the truck disappeared.

Toby stepped out and joined him. "Now that would be a good thing."

"I don't think Timber was expecting that."

"No, I don't imagine so, but it's a very good thing," Toby stated. "More than a good thing. Andy's a good man, and he knows what Timber's doing here is a good thing."

"A lot of people wouldn't care whether it's a good thing or not."

"Nope, and that's why Andy's special in that way. Plus, Timber and Andy have a bit of recent history that needs some smoothing over, some things that Andy feels guilty for. He's also very aware he's about to go over the rainbow to meet his wife, and Mariana Killerman was a force to be reckoned with in her day."

Burke looked at him. "Why does it sound like he's off-loading?"

"Andy's dying. He's got cancer."

"Oh, crap."

"So, the Killerman ranch has been broken into pieces, and, if he can't sell a lot of the leftover stuff, such as the equipment, it will likely end up at auction," Toby explained. "So Timber getting it is really the best answer for a lot of it."

"It's a great answer, isn't it?" Burke agreed.

"Plus, it allows the Killermans to save face and to not

have to deal with too much family garbage."

"Will there be family garbage?"

"Yeah, there could be," Toby stated, with distaste in his tone. "His son Max and his grandson Brian—who hurt Danny, his wife's pet—kidnapped Tiffany and caused all kinds of hell before Max died in a shootout with the local authorities. Not to mention that the military was after him too. Brian got lucky, getting to choose between prison or a tour or two with the military."

"I heard about Danny but had no idea about the rest," Burke muttered. "Not a nice thing in anybody's book."

"Plenty of bad feelings to go around because of Max Killerman and what he did to Tiffany, not to mention what Max did to everyone else in his life. An awful lot of guilt is mixed in there too. Andy knew Max had to be taken down, but it was still hard on everyone concerned. Apparently Andy's decided that, if he can help out, he'll try as much as he can."

"Which is absolutely lovely," Burke noted. "Now we just need to confirm there's a machine shed for everything to go in."

Toby frowned at him, then at the surrounding buildings, and groaned. "I didn't think of that."

"No, and that's one of the reasons we need the white-board and some organization to get the projects moving along here, without having to go back and fix things."

"And yet things are moving," Toby clarified, shaking his head. "Just not quite efficient enough is what you're telling me. Jesus, I'm getting too old for this shit."

"You are joking, right? I've seen you helping all around here."

"I suspected that would be your answer," he replied,

with a smile. "However, the deal with Andy is in progress, with whiteboards coming, so we'll continue to make good time and to do the best we can. Yet I suspect we'll need to start thinking about that machine shed."

With that, the two men looked around the place and discussed possible options for its location. They certainly wouldn't make decisions without Timber here, but it seemed as if somebody needed to get ideas started on this.

By the time Timber returned, a broad smile on his face, he looked over at them and declared, "We've got quite a bit of equipment to move over."

Burke smiled at him and asked, "And where are you planning to put it?"

"I don't know," he confessed, frowning, as he looked around. "I really hadn't put any machine shop in here as a consideration. Andy does have one of those big metal sheds, but I don't know how hard it would be to deconstruct it and to move it over here."

"And I guess the property line didn't include it, *huh*?" Burke asked, still smiling.

Timber turned to him and laughed. "No, and that's another thing we need to do. Get that new addition fenced."

"It's not fenced?"

"Not completely. One section where we need to add in fencing will cut it off from his land," Timber explained, "and will join it up to ours."

"Sounds good," Burke replied. "In the meantime, let's just keep things moving forward, and we'll deal with the additional fencing and the machine shop too."

Storage for the equipment was the conversation at dinnertime, and everybody had bits and pieces to suggest. There was consensus on one good solid location, but that shop would need a solid floor, and a solid floor meant concrete. Slabs of wood for a floor would deteriorate over time. Concrete was the best, but that would mean bringing out framers, getting it framed up, and bringing out a cement truck.

Shirley added her two bits worth as well. "I think the biggest issue is the fact that this is an awful lot of equipment, and it's very important to keep it safe, so if you have a location in mind, one consideration is whether or not it's close enough that we could put a water line to it. I can't imagine any scenario where you wouldn't need water in the machine shop. So that would make it a top priority to get accomplished faster."

Timber sighed as he looked over at her. "That's the thing. We have an awful lot of projects deemed as top priorities."

She smiled and nodded. "Did you get the whiteboards?"

"I did, as a matter of fact," Timber declared. "And I'm starting to feel as if I really could benefit from seeing that visual project list myself."

"Yep," she agreed, "and you will need something else." With that, she handed him a recorder.

"What's this for?" he asked.

"I need to get access to the most information I can. It's a matter of your sitting down and talking to me, like a brain dump onto this recorder of every plan you have for this place. Then I'll send it to my phone and start putting everything up on the whiteboard."

He frowned at the recorder. "I didn't even think about that," he muttered.

"This just happens to be one of the easiest ways for information to move from person to person," she stated, with a shrug. "And this way requires the least amount of time for you. So, grab a coffee, sit down on the porch, and let's start recording. Actually I would highly suggest we do this as a group, so we can keep track of what's happening for everybody."

He looked over at her and frowned. "The coffee sounds good, but somebody promised me cinnamon buns."

"Yeah, … well, somebody promised me whiteboards too," she countered.

"I got the whiteboards," he protested.

"And I got the cinnamon buns." She smiled broadly.

At that, Toby came over with a huge tray of still-warm cinnamon buns.

Immediately silence filled the room, as everybody just sniffed the air.

With a heartfelt sigh, Timber whispered, "Oh, this is freaking perfect." He started to reach for one, only to have Dwight hand him a plate.

"Let's not be complete Neanderthals. You'll have icing all over your hands and everything else if you don't use a plate." He quickly served up a round of cinnamon buns to everyone gathered here.

Burke watched as everybody eyed the remaining cinnamon buns, realizing they didn't have to rush; there would be at least another one for each of them, and he smiled over at Shirley. "You done good."

She beamed. "It's a simple-enough thing," she admitted, "and it does seem to make people happy."

"It might be simple to you, but it's quite a morale booster here," Dwight declared, as he joined them, carrying a cup of coffee and his own cinnamon bun.

She looked back at him and smiled. "You do a great job

with the meals."

He shrugged. "Yeah, but I'm not a good hand at baking fancy stuff."

"That's hardly fancy," she protested. "It's just cinnamon buns."

"Yeah, that's what I mean," he pointed out. "On the other hand, I'm pretty good at making bread."

"Oh, there's a lot to be said for homemade bread," she stated, with a happy sigh. "I haven't made bread in a very long time."

"If you want to start some in the morning, we can get going on that too," he suggested, with a smile.

"Do you happen to have a sourdough starter?" she asked.

"I do," he replied, "but I just started it a few days ago. In fact, you had sourdough-starter flapjacks for breakfast."

"That's what I wondered," she said with a nod. "They did have that *sourdough-y* taste."

"Yeah, that was them," Dwight confirmed. "So, as of tomorrow there's sourdough bread—or the next day."

She nodded. "I guess out here in the heat, it's hard to imagine the time frame."

"I'll give it a shot tomorrow," he replied, "or at least that is the plan. However, things are kind of busy, so if you feel like getting up and getting something started, it's all yours. But don't forget that you'll be working on that whiteboard all day too."

"Yes." She rubbed her hands together with glee. "I'll have to get out there and help muck too. An awful lot of things to be done."

He just smiled as she looked around, trying to figure out how that would all come together. When her phone buzzed against her leg, she hesitated, looked down, then immediately put it away again.

Burke looked over at her. "Silvia again?"

She shrugged and then nodded. "Yeah." She rolled her eyes. "It's not easy to keep ignoring her."

"And yet—"

"I know. I know," she said, with a wave of her hand. "I don't really have any way of dealing with her except to try to keep hiding," she admitted, with a snort.

"And hiding is okay too," he murmured.

"Is it?" she asked, giving him an odd look. "It feels like cheating."

Surprised, Timber glared at her. "No, it's not," he stated. "There's a time for offense, and there's a time for defense. You are in retreat mode right now, and, until we have answers and a way forward, that's where you should stay. Besides, you convinced me that I really need these whiteboards, so I don't dare let you run off now."

She laughed. "I'm grateful to have a way to be useful," she shared, "because I was feeling very much like a charity case, and that's not what I want to be."

"Charity or not, everybody needs a haven once in a while," Timber declared, "and that's what we are, a haven."

"Thank you," she said, with all sincerity. And then she looked at the recorder in his hand and began, "Now, tell me specifically what it is that you need done at the bunkhouse." When he looked at her, she flipped the switch on the recorder in his hand and added, "I'm starting with that because I'm thinking it might have the least amount of work to be done."

Some of the men laughed. "You might be thinking that, but you would be thinking wrong. The bunkhouse needs a fair bit."

"Sure," she conceded, "but I'm not sure it's as much as a lot of the other places, so let's get started."

The next three hours consisted of a lively back-and-forth discussion on to-do projects. When she could see that Timber was getting fed up, she took the recorder from him and suggested, "I'll get started with this."

"Okay," he said. "You think you've got something there we can work with?"

"I've definitely got something I can work with," she stated, with a smile. "The question is how much more I will need to hassle you about?"

"A lot," he muttered, with a groan. "I saw that one coming from a mile away."

# CHAPTER 12

THE PATTERN HELD like that for the next couple days, with evening discussions about the two whiteboards, as Shirley quickly organized all the different projects and all the different buildings, including the addition of a machine shop. Yet it was just a start. She needed to get out her laptop and start a new project spreadsheet to do it properly. She had project management software that would organize the details beautifully. The whiteboards were for the men, but they couldn't begin to handle the full scope of the integrated jobs.

As soon as Timber had seen that, he just groaned. "This will be insane."

"Of course it's insane," she agreed, with a knowing cackle. "All good things take work." He glared at her, and she just laughed. "And I know I'm the one who'll keep pushing and organizing this, but I'm not trying to be a pain in the butt."

"Yes, you are," he declared, and then he laughed. "But you did deliver on the cinnamon buns."

"It's brownies today," she muttered absentmindedly. The men stopped, looked at her, and she shrugged. "I just thought maybe you guys could use a break from cinnamon buns."

But when they continued to stare at her, she started to laugh. "Maybe I was wrong about that. Maybe there is no break needed in any way, shape, or form from cinnamon buns," she stated, starting to giggle.

Burke was absolutely loving how well she had fit into the place and how everyone was accepting and open to having her here. And she had very quickly made herself useful with the animals, but very much so when it came to organizing the charts—and to baking cinnamon buns.

She also carried a notepad that she was constantly making notes on.

When Burke asked her about it, she explained, "The two whiteboards are really just a start. Honestly, we would need quite a few more to do it right, so I'm trying to avoid that expense. I'm using my software for the bulk of the information and then the whiteboards are for the summaries as a visual for the men."

"And all those notes you are taking?"

"So … I'm constantly keeping notes on the side, rewriting things. Plus, I've got separate spreadsheets for each one of these individual buildings," she added. "It's really a matter of prioritizing the jobs. So that's what I'm doing."

He just stared at her. "That sounds absolutely fabulous."

"That's good," she said, "because I'm not sure everybody else feels that way."

He smiled and added, "Doesn't matter, this is the job."

"I know," she agreed, "and it's also partly why this job isn't something I really want to do longterm because not everybody appreciates being told what to do."

"Of course they don't," he said, with a smile, "but that doesn't matter, at least not here, because everybody knows what you're trying to do is keep Timber organized so his dream project, this Haven, comes to life."

"And he was doing a great job with getting his thoughts

down on the recorder," she shared. "Honestly, with the amount of work, with the various projects and all the stuff that had to happen so fast, that is where the problem came in. Without being able to track and to keep things in some sort of alignment and on schedule, it just all went to hell."

"That is exactly what happened," Burke admitted. "Seems three dozen or more men showed up initially, and then a handful or more showed up, and another bunch stayed, with some leaving and others coming back," Burke recapped, with a laugh. "At which point I showed up."

She smiled. "As long as everybody is helping, it's huge. Things are getting done, and that's really where the bottom line is."

"Things are getting done," he agreed, with a nod, "and we're all very happy to give Timber a hand."

When a weird howl split the air, everybody froze. Timber got up, walked over to the side of the front porch, and stared out into the evening. They had resumed their positions outside for another lively discussion on the work and what needed to be done, what had been done, what she could move off the whiteboard list, and what else got added on. As soon as one job got finished, it seemed to create twenty-seven more. As soon as those got dealt with, there were always more to take their place.

Burke walked over to join Timber and stared out into the darkness. "Any idea what that was?" he asked Timber.

"It was a wildcat," he replied calmly.

"Not Billy Bob?"

"No, Billy Bob's not here right now, so I'm not exactly sure what it was."

"But you don't like it?"

He turned and stared at him. "No, I don't like it at all."

Then he rejoined the men gathered around.

The discussion returned to work and to the issues people were having on various aspects of their tasks, but they had changed in tenor, and the conversation rapidly wound down.

When Timber got up and casually moved over to the side of the front porch again, everybody stopped and waited.

One of the men asked, "Is it safe to head to our bunks?"

"Give it a few minutes, will you?" Timber suggested.

The men just stayed where they were, but Shirley asked, "You guys all seem to be okay with whatever is going on out there. Could somebody fill me in?" Her voice was low and hesitant.

Toby looked at her intently. "That was a sign of distress," he explained. "When it comes to animals here, that is not something we ignore."

"Of course not. The horses are all in the barn, and I'm not sure what animal that would have been," she said, looking at them curiously.

"That's one of the things that makes this place special, since it could be any number of different things," Toby replied. "But, if Timber says it's a bobcat, mountain lion, wildcat, or something along that line, you can pretty well expect him to be right."

Even as they watched, Timber walked down the front steps and out to the edge of the fencing, where he stayed for a long moment. When he slowly made his way back, he looked over at the men. "Something out there is injured and needs help," he shared, "but it'll take a bit for that animal to get comfortable enough to come in."

"Of course," she muttered, frowning.

Timber added, "Which means everybody needs to be on high alert and to stay close, you hear me? Don't head out on your own at any point in time over the next day or so."

She just looked at him but didn't say anything.

Burke nodded and replied, "Will do, and, if you need a hand, let me know."

Timber frowned, looking around, "Yeah, I might. … I'm not sure." Then he stopped and added, "Did we make allowances for any rooms for wild animals?"

"Only in the treatment centers," Toby replied.

"We may have to do some rough field medicine," one of the men suggested to them. "Though we're not sure what's even going on yet."

"Were traps ever used on this land?" Burke asked.

"I hope not," Timber snapped, as he swore, "but that's something that needs to be noted, so we can ask Andy about it."

"I've got that marked down," Shirley noted, "and I sure hope the answer is no."

"You'll find that, for most places around here, it'll be a yes," Toby replied, with a nod. "And that really could be what we're looking at now."

With that, Timber walked a little closer to the area in question, staring out into the darkness.

Burke found it unnerving. Yet he was reassured because his friend appeared not disinterested, but not bothered by it either. Simply cautious. When Burke heard a weird low hum, he realized it was coming from Timber himself. As he listened, he could sense an almost soothing tone to it. He edged closer and closer to Timber.

When Timber heard howling, he stopped humming and asked, "Burke, you want to come give me a hand?"

The two men followed the wails and found a large mountain cat. A trap was clamped on its leg, hampering the big cat's ability to walk. It was otherwise free but could hardly walk with the trap on him.

"Good God, we'll need some tools for this," Burke muttered.

"I'm trying to figure out what would be best."

Burke looked at it for a moment. "I've got an idea." Then he quickly headed to the woodshop and came back almost immediately with pliers, two pry bars, and a couple other tools he thought might be necessary.

Timber took one look and nodded. "That should do it." As they both stepped closer to the big cat, Timber added, "We'll need to keep our energy very calm, very stable, very relaxed. You can't move suddenly or challenge him by looking at him too much."

Understanding exactly what Timber was saying, Burke just nodded, then replied, "If you can work on the trap, I can work on releasing the paw."

"Good enough," Timber replied.

And it wasn't easy by any means, but, using these tools, Timber managed to pry open the trap, and very quickly Burke had the big cat's paw free. The mountain cat stared at him, the paw dripping with blood. Burke frowned. "That will need treatment."

That's when Shirley appeared behind him. "I've got a dose of antibiotics here and some medical tape and gauze and antibiotic powder," she explained.

"Good," Burke replied, then turned to Timber. "What are the chances of her putting on a bandage?"

"We won't force the cat to stay, but he's lying right here, not attempting to run, so let's try this." When she stepped up closer, Timber told Burke, "Use the pry bars to keep that paw just where it is."

SHIRLEY MOVED AS slow as anybody had ever seen and gradually knelt beside the big cat, giving him time to adjust to her presence. Mustering a great faith in wildlife, she then sprinkled the antiseptic powder all over the paw. She struggled to wrap it and was afraid that the bandage wouldn't seal very nicely.

Timber watched and whispered, "He's not fighting you. In my experience, … once they realize you're helping, they're willing to let you, as long as you don't do anything to upset the apple cart."

"We do need to give him the shot of antibiotics though," she reminded Timber, holding out the syringe.

"Let me try." Timber managed to inject the antibiotic into the large cat, surprising them all.

The cat howled and hissed but stayed exactly where it was. She quickly checked the bandage once more, and then, with a word from Timber, they both stepped back ever-so-slightly. The large cat eyed Timber, who remained close by. The big cat flexed its paw a time or two, then slowly stood up and raced several steps away. There, it stopped and looked back at him.

"He's walking at least," Burke noted.

"Yes, but why is he stopping and looking at us?" she asked in confusion.

Timber explained, "He's just making sure we're still here, that everything is okay."

And, with that, the large cat quickly disappeared into the darkness.

Timber grabbed the trap with a growl. "Gotta ask Andy how many more of these we need to disarm and toss."

She let out a shaky breath. "Any chance the wildcat will come back and let us change his bandage?"

Timber laughed. "Not a hope," he declared, with a smile. "Chances are, depending on how well you put it on, it'll stay there until he can chew it off."

"He shouldn't be able to do that for a little bit," she noted, "at least long enough for it to heal."

"He may have it off within seconds, depending on how much it's bothering him," Timber shared. "But we've done what we can do, and right now that's literally all there is to be done." With that he let out a sigh, looked at the two of them, and nodded. "Thanks for the help."

She smiled at him. "No thanks necessary. Opportunities like that are what you're doing this for, right? How do you manage to keep injectable antibiotics on hand?"

He looked over at her and smiled. "Tiffany, my girl-friend. She is our local vet and keeps us stocked up on supplies. I've also had some field training as a medic, so it's all well recorded and legit."

She patted him on the back and muttered, "Good job."

He laughed and asked, "Why do I get the *good job* pat on the back?"

"Choosing a veterinarian for a girlfriend," Burke quipped.

"Oh, shush," she teased, with a smile, turning back to Timber. "Because, without your calm energy, we would never have been able to approach that cat," she explained. "It's only because of you that we could help him."

"Let's hope we don't need to do it anymore."

"I think he'll be fine," she shared, as she looked into the darkness, where he'd disappeared. "Hopefully, if he needs more help, he'll know to come back. The fact that he let us help amazes me."

"Not just that he knew to come in the first place," Burke clarified, "but that he was willing."

"Exactly," she stated, with a smile. And, with that, she looked at Burke and Timber. "I really am grateful that you're letting me stay here. It's given me a completely new viewpoint on life, one that was sorely needed."

He smiled at her. "Hey, as long as you keep making cinnamon buns, you're gold here."

She laughed. "So the brownies will pass muster too maybe?"

He shrugged. "Maybe. It all depends on how good they are."

"Oh, they're great," she stated, a grin on her face. "But you can always tell me about it tomorrow."

# CHAPTER 13

ARLY THE NEXT morning, as Shirley poured herself some coffee, her phone vibrated again, and she sighed, letting it go to voice mail. A few minutes later, she pulled it out and hit Play on the recorded message.

"You've got to help me," Silvia shrieked through the phone. "He'll kill me. You've got to help me. You have to. Ever since you left, he's been so angry and upset, all because of you. He was counting on that money to get us through," she screamed into the phone. "You've got to help me." And then the message went deathly silent.

Shirley stared down at the phone, only vaguely aware she was on the verge of collapsing. Strong hands went around her to guide her to a chair.

She stared up blindly at Burke, who placed her coffee in front of her, then squatted and held her hand. "Easy," he whispered, "take it easy." She couldn't even speak, as her mouth opened and then closed. He nodded. "I know, it's a shock."

She grappled with that. "A shock," she cried out. "How is that a shock? That's not a shock. That's like ..." And then she just blanked out.

He continued to rub her hands and just helped her deal with the moment.

Timber walked over and joined them, looking concerned.

"Somebody needs to bring me back to earth here," she muttered.

"Would she do this to set you up?" Timber asked.

She blinked at him in shock, and it took her a moment to realize what he was asking.

"Oh God," she whispered, her shoulders sagging. "I don't even know."

"Right," Timber declared, "and that's one of the first things we have to figure out. It comes down to whether this is her just trying to flush you out or if she's really in trouble. Obviously, if she's in trouble, she needs help."

She grasped what he was saying, but it had been such a shock to hear her sister's panicked voice like that. "I don't know," she whispered. "I really don't know."

"But you are afraid of the boyfriend. Frankie, right?"

"Yes. I'm absolutely terrified of him," she admitted. "And, for good reason, because he's definitely frightening."

"Good enough," Timber stated calmly.

Burke stroked her cheek. "You need to relax a little bit." She took several deep breaths, and he nodded approvingly. "Do that a few more times," he said calmly, "and we'll go from there."

She realized he had said *we*, not just her. Her shoulders sagged in relief. "Dear God, I don't know what I would do if I was alone right now."

Burke snorted. "You would have bolted and already been halfway into town, calling her as you went."

She nodded. "I would have because she's still my sister, even though I know we have all kinds of problems with her, and she's pure trouble." She winced. "I can't deal with the fact that she might be in trouble, and I am the cause of it."

At that, both men glared at her, with Burke stating firm-ly, "You are not the cause of this."

She sat here, blinking at them, still in a daze.

Toby walked over, slammed his hand down on the table, and snapped, "You are not to blame for any of this."

"But if I had given her the money …"

"And then what? After you let her take all the money you've got, then what? They would still be broke very quickly, especially considering the rate they're going through it," Toby stated, staring at her. "You need to let go of that guilt. Let go of that misplaced generosity. It seems to me that whole family has had you wrapped up in guilt for a lifetime."

"He's right," Burke agreed, taking her hand in his. "Enough is enough."

She swallowed at the vehemence in Toby's tone and then took a slow, calming breath. "Do you think so?" she asked Burke.

"I know so," Burke declared. "Absolutely no way this behavior can continue, and I'm sorry, but the only way she'll stop is if somebody stops her. I know that isn't what you want to hear, but—"

"I know," she interrupted, nodding. "Intellectually I get that," she admitted, "and I do understand, but emotionally I'm just not quite there yet."

"Has your father been jailed before?"

"Yes, but it was quite a while ago."

"Do you trust him?"

"No, not at all."

Toby looked at her and then slowly nodded. "You really don't have anybody, do you?"

"No," she whispered. "I never have. It's always been a hard slog to sort out whether they're lying or cheating or whatever else they're doing, so I just stayed clear of them as much as I could, but she's still my sister."

"She is, but this could be the end of that sibling love."

She looked at him in confusion. "What do you mean?"

"If this is a trap, or if she's trying to flush you out so they can get your money or whatever it is they think they'll get from you, it's sure to be a one-way ticket to the end of that relationship."

She knew it herself and nodded. "Yes, it would be. ... It's just hard for me to believe she would do that."

Timber looked over at Burke, who shook his head and added, "It's not hard for me to believe it at all."

She looked up and winced. "I know, but that's because she's already caused you some difficulty," she murmured. "She's never hurt me."

"*Yet*," he clarified, "but she's done a lot to hurt your circumstances ... or tried to."

She sighed. "I really don't think I can deal with the fact that you think she might be trying to trap me."

"It's a possibility, and it's also a possibility that Frankie's trying to trap you. You said you didn't trust him, right?"

"No, I don't. Not at all."

"Okay, so do you think that Frankie would use Silvia to get to you?"

She frowned as she thought about it. "Yes, I think he would, but I don't know what he would want from me."

"You took the money away, right?" Timber asked.

"I didn't take it away," she clarified, with a sniff. "I removed her ability to access it."

"Is there any doubt that the money isn't just yours?" Toby asked.

"No, ... God no," she declared, staring at Toby. "Burke

already knows this, but I'm the one who earned it. It was in my bank account, and Silvia's name was never on it and was never intended to be on it. That's just my checking account, not my investment account. I don't know what they would do if they knew about that."

"And you already know that she was quite prepared to steal from you."

"Yes," she confirmed, "and honestly, I've gotten accustomed to that because she's done it before."

His jaw worked as he heard her, and he glanced over at the others. Toby just shook his head, got up, and poured himself another cup of coffee.

"I guess I've been normalizing that the whole time, haven't I?" she asked.

"Yes," Burke stated, "you have been, and you've probably been doing it because *it's family*, and because it's family, we tend to tolerate all kinds of stuff we wouldn't let others get away with."

She closed her eyes and nodded. "So, what am I supposed to do now?" She stared down at her phone. "I can't ignore this."

At that point, Timber stepped forward. "Then you meet her, but you do not meet her alone, and you do not put yourself in any position where you could be taken captive."

She stared at him in shock. "Are you saying you think they would hurt me?" she cried out, staring at him in horror.

He looked at her, his face grim. "I remember how stressed and frightened you were when you initially got here. And it's a very slim line to kidnapping you from what they've already been doing. If holding you captive means getting access to your bank account, your investments, or whatever else they seem to think that they'll get access to, it's a pretty minor step, considering the various illegal acts they've already been committing."

"But …" She stopped and frowned.

Timber continued. "Just because they haven't been caught doesn't mean that what they're doing is legal."

"No, I know that," she whispered. "I do realize that much."

"Then you need to take it one step further and to realize that the worst-case scenario is that they could literally use you for their own benefit, and that is not something you can afford to have happen."

"No, I can't."

"And you already know you don't trust Frankie," Burke added, "and, if he has a good grip on Silvia, then you really can't afford to meet them at all."

She winced, then suggested, "You can phone them. You can see what the problem is and whether you believe her or not, and then we can go from there." She pulled out her phone and started to hit Redial.

Burke grabbed her hand to slow her process. "You need to remember all the things she has already done, not just to me but to you."

"Why?"

"So you don't just cave when she starts to cry," he replied. "I know myself how good she is at making you think her world is completely collapsing and that you are the only one who can help her."

"I need to help her," Shirley stated, staring at him steadily. "I don't want to get in Frankie's clutches, and I certainly don't want to have any problem with him." She winced at that thought and then shrugged. "If she's not lying, not making this up, then it is quite possible that he's hurting her, and that is something I could never forgive myself if I ignored it."

"I get that, but remember all that she is and all that she has already done. That's all we're saying," Burke repeated, as Toby and Timber nodded.

"It's a plea for help, and, as much as I don't trust her—God help me, I know I don't trust her—but how am I supposed to get past that level of pain? If it was your brother or sister, and you didn't trust them, but they were crying out with a call for help, what would you do?"

Toby nodded. "I would contact them and see if it was for real," he said, "but I wouldn't go by my own judgment on something like this because I would know I was too emotionally attached and couldn't be objective."

She stared at him and winced. "Right, message received."

He sighed. "We're not trying to be mean, but we're trying to be reasonable, and being reasonable is not easy. But I also get that right now she's got you completely bamboozled into believing that she's hurting, and, because it could be possible, you can't take the chance."

Timber added, "I agree with Toby. If your sister is being held captive by somebody who could hurt her, that isn't something any of us would ignore. … However, we already know that she's a con artist and that her word can't be trusted. Not only her words but her actions, her deeds, her voice, and certainly not her partner."

"I know. God help me." She looked at Burke. "What do you think I should do?"

"I think you should call her and turn the Speaker on so all of us can hear. Then we'll judge the sincerity in her tone and will make a decision on whether we believe her or not," he suggested. "But you also need to be prepared that she'll want to meet right away or she'll want you to send her money."

"I'm not sending her money," Shirley stated. "She has money."

"What do you mean, she has money?" Burke asked.

"Well, … as far as I know, she has money, *yours*. I don't know if she has burned through it all or not, but there was money at one point in time." She sighed. "And maybe she has none. I don't know. Maybe that's why she's calling me. Who knows with her."

"All I know for sure is that I don't trust her." Burke stared her down.

"No, of course not. That's something else I have to keep in mind. You are biased against her. While I know and appreciate that you're looking out for me, you're also coming from a position where your trust has been smashed."

He smiled at her. "That's very true," he agreed calmly. "Yet I would very much like to think myself capable of being objective."

"Whereas I'm not?" she challenged.

He looked at her and shook his head. "No, you're not. You're here because of her, after all."

"Oh God." She gasped, as she looked around and realized the truth of what they were saying.

"You lost your job, and you're sitting here because you needed a place to hide for a few days," Timber added. "Let's not forget what—or who—drove you to that."

Tears came to her eyes, and she scrubbed them away. "I don't know what to do," she muttered, her tone calmer as she realized the truth of what they were saying.

"Nothing brings us around the bend more than family," Toby declared, as he filled up her coffee cup. "I'm making breakfast, so you get yourself in a position to start eating, do you hear me?"

She looked over at him. "I'm sorry, but I don't think I can eat right now."

"You better, because your stomach won't handle all this added chaos without food," he stated, scrunching up his nose. "Your body needs fuel, like it or not. The stress alone will make you sick."

She groaned. "And that's not what I need right now."

Timber pointed out, "You also haven't called her." When she stared down at the phone, he continued. "And you know why."

"I do know why, … because I don't trust her. And I feel like such a horrible person for saying so," she whispered.

"And I'll repeat what Toby just told you. Family can chew us up into a million pieces and then spit us out," Timber stated. "There is nothing like the pull of needing to help somebody who's hurting and in need. The trouble is, in this instance, we don't know if it's a real call for help, or if it's just an attempt to flush you out."

"Flush me out?"

"You've been hiding, haven't you?"

"He's right," Dwight agreed from the sidelines.

"That he is," Burke declared.

Timber nodded. "You are here in hiding, and she knows you must have gone to ground somewhere. She doesn't know where, and we don't want her finding that out either," Timber declared. "Under no circumstances do I want the animals disturbed or put under any added pressure or nastiness from Silvia and Frankie," he stated calmly.

"Oh God, no." She stared at Timber. "That would devastate me." She turned to look out at the animals grazing calmly in the pastures. "I haven't mucked out the stalls yet," she noted, staring out into the yard.

"And that's fine," Burke replied, patting her hand. "I'll do it today, just like I planned to do it any day that I don't have help. What is important right now is that you sort out this thing with your sister."

She gave a broken laugh. "How the hell am I supposed to do that when I don't even know what the truth of this is?"

"And that's where the problem is," Toby pointed out, as he placed a plate of hash browns, bacon, and eggs in front of her. "Telling the truth from the fiction, that's the challenge."

"And maybe your sister is in trouble," Timber suggested. "You know we're here for you, and, if she's not in trouble, and this is who she is—someone who preys on her own sister—then we'll help you put her behind bars. Let's rope Richard into this. He's a local detective we've had to call on before."

She looked over at him and sighed. "I don't know how I got so lucky as to find you guys, but I've got to tell you that my sister, if she's angry and upset, … Silvia can be pretty ugly."

"And when you say, *pretty ugly?*" Timber asked her.

"Vindictive, mean, like … burning down the barn is not something I would put past her," she explained, hesitantly looking over at Timber.

"And that's one of the reasons we want to confirm she doesn't come here," he said, "because that attitude is not what we need here. There's a reason we call it *the Haven*."

"Of course," she muttered. "I should leave anyway. I'll pack up my bags right after I finish eating," she offered, and then she pushed back the plate. "I'm not even hungry so I'll just go pack up now."

"And where do you think you're going, after you pack up?" Timber asked.

"I, … I don't know." She hung her head. "But I don't want to bring them here."

He smiled the gentlest of smiles at her. "I don't want to keep them away and then put you in danger," he clarified. "However, I will protect my place and my animals, and the end result could potentially look nothing like what your sister is hoping for."

"No, it won't," Shirley agreed, "because she's not used to people who fight back. She's …" She turned to Burke and shook her head. "Silvia's a user."

Burke nodded. "That she is," he confirmed, rolling his eyes. "Nevertheless, if she's in trouble, then we need to help her."

Her eyes filled with tears, and she nodded. "Thank you. Thanks for saying that, but we want to keep her away from here," she added.

Timber nodded. "That would be the best, so you'll go meet her in town." He frowned. "I'll send you in with somebody from the group here."

At that, two of the men immediately volunteered, and she looked at them in surprise, turning to Burke instead.

"It's better to *not* be Burke," Timber noted, "because Burke will set off Silvia and might give her suspicions as to why she's in trouble right now in terms of the police."

"Oh God," Shirley muttered. "I didn't even think of them."

Timber noted, "She should be out there getting picked up by the locals. I'm not sure why she hasn't been, and that may just be dumb luck so far. However, I'll be asking Richard that question myself." Timber shook his head. "We know that can absolutely happen. Sometimes it seems the criminals get a free pass from the universe, when really it's just a matter of time."

Burke nodded at that. "I would say so too. And I'm not against going in with Shirley, that's for sure, but I want to know where you will meet her because there's absolutely no reason for the cops not to pick her up."

She looked at him, with a quizzical gaze. "And that would imply that I'm setting her up," she said, with a wince.

He nodded. "It would."

Timber sat down beside her and reminded her, "You've already gone to the police."

"I know. I know, and it's the right thing to do," she admitted, with a groan. "But it's also … I, … I …" She sighed.

And Timber finished her sentence for her. "You don't want to be involved anymore."

"I would hate to have her get picked up because of me, and yet I should be happy that she's getting picked up because of me," she cried out in confusion and frustration. "There's absolutely no reason for her to get away with what she's doing."

"And maybe what she's doing isn't good for anybody, but, if she's in trouble, and you have the cops as a backup," Burke pointed out, "then at least you'll have some backup yourself, in case the boyfriend is there."

"Oh, he'll be there," she stated.

At that, Timber looked at her and asked, "In that case, why would you go?"

She stared at him. "I have to," she replied simply.

"Then we'll send a couple men with you," Timber said, "and we'll contact the police and let them know where Silvia and Frankie will be."

"And you also know," Shirley added in frustration, "that, if the police show up, and I'm there, she'll think it was me."

"Maybe she needs to. Maybe she needs to understand that enough is enough," Timber pointed out.

"I get it," Burke interjected. "You don't want to face her, and you don't want to face the consequences of having turned her in, but the consequences are hers, not yours, for her actions. She's the one who put herself in this spot to begin with, and, if she asks for money to run, and you give it to her, after you've already contacted the police, that won't look great for you either."

She frowned at him. "I didn't even think of that."

"No, that's because you're just reacting. And that's not what we need right now. We need your brain turned on."

She closed her eyes, settled back, and, without even being aware of it, she opened her mouth when Burke put a fork of food in front of her, and she chewed, not even seeing it as he did it a few more times. Then he put the fork in her hand and said, "I'll come too, but I'll stay behind you, and you'll go in with one of the men Timber has suggested."

She looked at him and nodded. "That could work."

"We'll just be a backup in case there's a problem," the burly veteran added from her side.

She wasn't sure of his name but thought it was Jaxon.

"I am, however," Timber declared, "contacting Detective Richard Martin and asking him if there's any progress on Silvia. If not, why not?"

"We gave him all kinds of leads to go pick them up," Burke stated, "and the fact that they haven't picked them up is where the challenge is at."

She winced. "It goes along with my sister always having luck on her side. It's always been a frustration, but that is her and always has been."

"Yes, but that luck doesn't stay around forever, and at some point they'll get run to ground, and what we don't want is for there to be a standoff at the end of the day anywhere, but especially not here at the Haven for sure."

She stared at him, her eyes wide, realizing what he was saying. She closed her eyes and whispered, "No, that wouldn't be good."

"Would your father help or would he warn her? Would he say anything to her, or tell you anything about her?"

"He would probably tell me to fuck off," she replied, with a sudden sense of understanding. When they all stared, she shrugged. "He's really not a fan of mine."

"Of course not," Timber said, with a smile, "because, if you're not for him, you're against him, and that would be his motto."

"Yes, and Silvia has always been for him, so whatever she wanted, he would go out and steal from someone to get."

"And what about you?"

"No," she replied. "When I realized how he was getting the stuff for Silvia and that other people were literally losing it because of him, I refused to condone that. As soon as I told him how I thought about it, he got really angry," she shared. "That was one of the few times he beat me. After that? ... Well, you just learn to keep your mouth shut."

"Of course you do, and yet that's also not the way to live."

"No, it's not the way to live," she agreed, "but, when you're a kid, you don't have a choice, so you do whatever you can do to survive."

"And that's what you have to look at right now, as well. Your sister is doing whatever she can do to survive, but, in her mind, doing what she can do to survive has a whole different meaning than it does for you."

She stared at him and winced. "That is quite true. She has actively pointed out things that other people had that she wanted, and my father arranged to take it from them. He was so eager to get it for her that it just made me sick."

The other men stared at her in shock, then shook their heads. "That must be rough," Jaxon said, his voice grating.

She nodded. "High school was rough, and I left as soon as I could."

"And even then," Burke noted, "it probably wasn't fast enough."

"No, it wasn't nearly fast enough," she agreed. "How could it be? That upbringing? … All I've got to say is it's deadly."

"It is deadly, and it's harsh, and it's a lot of things, but you learned, and you moved on. None of that is your responsibility at this point. So just try to relax and let us help."

# CHAPTER 14

BURKE WASN'T AT all impressed with the idea of Shirley meeting Silvia, but he also could understand the panic at the thought of her sister being held against her will or being hurt by this boyfriend. Frankie did seem to be quite the asshole. Burke wanted a chance to go up against him, but that was not the way to handle this and something else he didn't need to deal with right now.

He did have some emotions that he still needed to deal with in terms of Silvia, and that would take him some time. He thought he'd already dealt with them, but instead they kept popping up, like now.

As he prepped to get ready, Timber came to him and asked, "Are you sure?"

He looked over at him and nodded. "Yeah, I'm sure."

"I'm sending Tommy with you, and Jaxon will be tailing her."

"Good enough, and do you have somebody else to go along with Jaxon?"

Timber smiled and nodded. "Absolutely. There are always men around who want a challenge,"

"I don't want to take anybody who's not ready for that kind of confrontation."

"Toby was jumping at the thought of having a chance to go," Timber shared, with a smile. "I'm not sure you're up for that either. Dwight isn't happy about missing out either."

"No, I think she would be upset if she thought either of them were coming, mostly just because she's scared and would want to confirm they would be safe."

Timber laughed at that. "Don't you underestimate those two. They may be older than the rest of us, but they're not that old, and they would be furious to hear you say that."

"I won't dare say it," he noted, with a smile, "and you're right. Dwight and Toby are not old and have done a hell of a lot more for all of us than most of us even realize."

"Absolutely. And right about now, you need somebody to watch your back."

"I know, and Tommy is a good fit. I want somebody to go in with her."

"I would normally send you, but Jaxon works better this time."

"I know, and I would be the first to go," Burke admitted, "if I thought I could stay hidden from view. Regardless I will still be one to go."

Timber pondered that and nodded. "That's not a bad idea. You could get to the meeting place well ahead of time and just stay in the background, so nobody could see you."

"And yet, if there's trouble," he pointed out, "I could hop out and get involved."

"Sure, but you'll do that anyway, won't you?"

He frowned at that, then slowly nodded. "If I needed to …"

"Right, so they'll find out you're there and that you are involved regardless."

"I hadn't thought of that," he muttered, "so …"

Timber frowned and suggested, "I can always come along."

"Anybody else?" Burke asked.

"Why? What's wrong with me?" Timber glared at him.

He snickered. "I'm pretty sure she would be the first one to say you need to get busy on that whiteboard update."

Timber glared. "You know that I would come just to get out of that, right?"

Burke burst out laughing and nodded. "I know you would, and she knows that too. Yet she also knows that you need to do the whiteboard work."

"Sure," he conceded, with a sigh. "But doing that isn't interesting at all, not when all this is going on."

"Nope, sure isn't," Burke replied, with a chuckle. "On the other hand, if you have anybody else and if anybody else wants to come, that would probably be better. We also need to know that the animals here are truly safe, and that means you need to stay and to keep watch. And keep your damn phone on."

At that Tommy stepped up. "I'm coming too. Jaxon and I have worked together pretty well before."

He looked at him and frowned. "It could get ugly."

"Yeah, it could," he said, with a smile. "I've done my time in the military too. I know exactly what ugly looks like."

"What I really don't understand is *ugly family*," Jaxon noted. "That's something I'm not used to, so it will be an education."

"Same for me," Tommy added.

"And not necessarily one you want," Timber warned him.

Jaxon smiled. "I did two tours," he replied. "I've seen all kinds of shit, but nothing is as mean or as ugly as family gone bad."

Burke nodded. "Particularly when it turns on itself. I understand why Shirley needs to check it out, but I also think that we need to be very careful. There is nothing about this scenario that I like."

Timber nodded. "Yeah, I'm betting it's a trap."

"But is it a trap by the boyfriend or a trap by the sister?" Burke asked.

The men stared at him, back at each other, and then shrugged. "No way to know."

"Which is why we have to go," Burke stated. "And I think you're right. If we go early, and I hide someplace, that would be a good answer in terms of keeping an eye on Shirley."

"I think it's a good answer too," Jaxon agreed.

"You ride with her," Burke urged Jaxon. "Keep her calm at least. Tommy and I will take your vehicle, if you're all right with that." Jaxon nodded. "Of course," Burke added, "this isn't even your fight."

"Technically, it's not yours either," Jaxon pointed out. "But she is doing the right thing. She's trying to help, and apparently the two of you are … friends?"

"Definitely friends," Burke admitted. "And potentially so much more than that, but to get involved with that family again …"

"I would risk it for her, if I were you," Timber suggested. "I haven't known Shirley for very long, but I've seen her around the animals, and I've watched her pitch in, helping, doing the right thing. I have to respect that. It won't be an easy road she has ahead of her, but we need to give her an opportunity to do what needs to be done, and that also means helping you get clear of the nightmare that her sister has caused you."

Burke nodded. "I would absolutely freaking love that. Did you get a hold of the detective?"

Timber shook his head. "With any luck we can sort this out before you even get back," Timber replied. "I'll keep trying to reach Richard. He is also a veteran, plus has worked with us locally."

"How about he just meets us at the park and sorts it out while we're there?" Jaxon suggested, with a sigh.

"And picks up Silvia and Frankie," Burke added. "That would be good."

"You really like that idea, don't you?" Jaxon asked.

"Yeah, wouldn't you?" he asked, with a snort. "Just think. All of this could be over and done with, and Shirley could come back and just relax for a bit."

Timber nodded at that. "I like the sound of that too, but my Spidey senses say this won't be settled easily."

Burke looked over at him and nodded grimly. "Yeah, your Spidey senses and mine are on the same page."

# CHAPTER 15

S HIRLEY STARED AT Burke over the hood of the vehicle. "You don't need to come," she cried out, checking her watch anxiously, "but I have to go."

"I'm coming," he declared. "There'll be three of us. Jaxon's riding with you, and Tommy and I are coming right behind you."

She frowned as she looked over Jaxon. "I don't … Do you really think that's necessary?" she asked, her voice fading, as she realized they thought there would be trouble.

Jaxon asked, "Why don't we confirm that there won't be trouble first, and then we won't have to worry about it?"

She took a slow, deep breath, trying to regain control over her emotions. Ever since she got that panicked phone call from Silvia, Shirley had been racing to get to her sister, and it just seemed as if everything had slowed down her progress. She'd already arranged with her sister to meet her at a certain location and had told the men where that was. But, when she realized that Burke was planning on coming too, she'd balked, knowing that her sister would throw a raging fit.

"She might very well throw a fit," he agreed, with a nod, "but, if you're in deep trouble, we don't want anything bad to happen to you."

"Right, I understand. … It's just the thought that we're

going in there, expecting something like that …"

"Not expecting," Timber clarified. "*Prepared,* just in case."

She looked over at him, seeing the reason and the calm attitude he displayed, and she slowly nodded. "Fine," she whispered. "From my point of view, I'm really, really hoping that nothing goes wrong."

"Of course," Timber replied. "We are too."

She winced and nodded. "But you're still expecting it, aren't you?"

He gave her a ghost of a smile. "Again, not expecting, but let's not get caught with our pants down."

"Right," she murmured. And with a nod toward the men, she announced, "Fine, but I'm leaving now."

"We're going ahead of you," interjected Burke, as he hopped into Jaxon's vehicle.

"Or you can just go with her," Timber noted. "Jaxon is good, but you would be even better."

"You know that'll just cause trouble."

"But it also might make Silvia and Frankie reconsider."

With that, a quick reshuffle happened, and Burke took over the wheel of Shirley's vehicle, having her scoot over to the passenger seat. Then Tommy and Jaxon went on ahead, taking Jaxon's vehicle.

"Do you really think we need all this?" Shirley asked, as they drove out. "Silvia called out for help."

"She did call out for help."

"You really don't like her, do you?"

He looked over at her and laughed. "It's not about whether I like her or not," he clarified, "but I'm also very aware of what games she can pull."

She winced. "And I shouldn't even be bringing it up to

you because you, of all people, are completely aware of what she's done."

"And what she's still likely to do to you this time," he pointed out. "You don't know who she is on the inside anymore because the person you knew would never have done this."

"No, she wouldn't have," she conceded, with a groan. "I just can't believe I'm even in this situation. What was the point of doing all this if it'll just cause me nothing but hell?"

He looked over at her and nodded. "For one thing you need to see with your own eyes if your sister is truly in trouble. For another thing, you're doing me a huge favor, which is also why I want to confirm that I'm there in case anything goes wrong."

She shook her head. "It's more likely to go wrong because you're there."

"Maybe," he agreed, with a nod. "However, I plan to stay hidden, unless you need me. If they try to kidnap you, I will make my presence known. So, if it comes to that, seeing me is definitely a possibility, but at least then she would know that I blamed her, and it would be out in the open."

"She'll be absolutely livid with me."

"Do you think she isn't already?"

She winced at that. "She'll get even more livid," she corrected. "There will be punishment, and somebody will have to pay for it."

He shook his head. "This isn't a normal way to live. You do know that, right?"

"What isn't?" she asked, distracted as she looked around at the trees. She frowned. "I don't even know what's wrong, but I feel a great sense of … panic."

"About your sister?" he asked.

She frowned as she thought about it. "I really don't know. It just feels … very wrong."

"It *is* very wrong," he stated. "A lot here is very wrong." He drove carefully and quickly, the other vehicle moving ahead of them at lightning speed.

Shirley noted, "I guess my car doesn't travel quite as fast as Jaxon's, does it?"

"No," Burke agreed, with a laugh, "it sure doesn't, and they're making good time."

She pointed. "They're disappearing off into the distance on us."

He smiled. "And that's okay. We all know the rendezvous spot, and they'll confirm when they get in position."

"I wonder why the sheriff's office hasn't picked them up yet?" she asked, as she stared out. "Maybe they don't care. Maybe it's just not enough of a case for them to give a crap about."

"And that's possible, but it's not likely. Still, it is something we have to consider."

"I don't want to consider anything," she muttered, "not with Frankie involved." When Burke didn't say anything, she looked over at him and asked, "You believe me, right?"

"Of course I believe you," he stated, glancing at her. "That's never been in doubt."

She breathed out a sigh of relief. "Thank you. I have to admit this whole thing's got me feeling particularly … unnerved."

"Stay calm. It will do you no good to let the fear take over."

"You've got a gorgeous place to sort yourself out, and a part of me is so jealous because you get to stay in a place where you're safe and where you don't have to watch every word you say and everything you do," she shared. "Plus the crappy little jobs I was doing, … they were terrible. Yet it didn't seem to matter. Anything and everything could go wrong, and it felt as if I was working in a minefield all the time."

"Sounds like it was time for a new job."

She snorted. "Whether it was or not, it absolutely is now because I don't have any choice."

"Just remember that Silvia did that too."

"And yet it's not as if I warned her about it."

He frowned at her. "Do you know many people you have to warn about proper behavior when you're at work?"

"No, but she's never been anybody who cared."

"I need you to think about this as we drive into town," he stated calmly. "Can you think of any instance where your sister thought about or helped you in any way at all?"

She winced. "You're really thinking she is doing something dastardly here, aren't you?"

"Dastardly?" he asked, his lips quirking at the old-fashioned term.

"I don't even know what to call it," she said, with a mirthless laugh. "I just know that boyfriend of hers is one scary son of a bitch."

"And that's why we're all moving forward," he stated, "because, if she is in *that* kind of trouble, we're all there to help her. She's obviously got a lot of issues, and hopefully she can square herself up and can move away from these cons. However, just because she has issues doesn't mean that she continues to get a free pass."

"I know," she muttered, "and I don't think she really gets that either. She's—"

"Has she ever been there for you?"

She frowned as she thought about it. "I don't know what you mean by *being there for me.*"

He sighed. "There aren't too many instances where that needs an explanation. Has she ever gone above and beyond to help you?"

"No, … I can't think of anything. It's always been me in trouble and her laughing from the sidelines, but I always felt as if maybe she was laughing because it was a self-preservation thing."

He pondered that for a long moment. "Are you okay with that? With her looking after herself to stay alive and well?"

"Yeah," she replied casually. "That's what people do, right?"

"No," he declared, "that's not what people do." She looked at him, and he shook his head. "I don't know very many people who would do something heartless at the expense of somebody else."

She shrugged. "Apparently we know a lot of different people."

"And that is true," he agreed. "If your sister was in trouble, would she go to your father?"

"Sure, she definitely would," she replied.

"So, why do you think she hasn't done so now?"

She frowned at that. "Maybe she couldn't get a hold of him."

"Would he agree with the boyfriend abusing her?"

She thought about that. "I don't think so. I can't imagine that would be something he would be okay with. He never beat her himself," she shared, thinking about it, "so I can't imagine that would be something he would be willing to accept now."

"And yet he hit you."

"A couple times," she nodded, "not always, not often, but yeah, … there were a few times." He just nodded, his jaw working. She added, "I can't get upset about that. I haven't had anything to do with him in a very long time."

"Good," he replied, "and yet, over this mess, you might need to."

"I don't know about that. I've done a lot to avoid dealing with him." Then she groaned. "Honestly, I'm not sure how to react right now."

"So don't. Just sit back, relax, and give yourself a chance to think. Give yourself a chance to even feel and to realize that we don't know what's going on. So a little bit of time and patience will help both of us."

She looked over at him. "Why do I always forget how nice you are?"

"Oh no, no, no, no, no," he said. "You don't get to put me in the nice category."

She started laughing. "Sorry, you're already in the nice category."

He groaned. "That's like being friend-zoned," he replied. "It's really terrible on a guy's ego."

"It's terrible on anybody's ego," she noted. "Not just guys. Being friend-zoned as a woman is rough if you wanted something different too."

"And yet," he pointed out, "I guess in a way it's a kindness if it's not something that the other person wants."

"That's what they say," she murmured. "Besides, I wasn't trying to friend-zone you. I was just trying to acknowledge how much you've done for me."

"Which is not an issue," he pointed out.

She smiled. "You keep saying that."

"And I mean it," he said. "I really do. I'm not here to cause you trouble."

"No, … maybe not, yet a lot of these issues are troublesome. I don't know how she'll react when she sees you."

"If we get there early enough," he pointed out, "she won't see me."

"Do you promise to stay out of sight and out of the way?"

"Only as long as things are going well," he clarified. "As soon as anything is not going well, then, no, all bets are off." She groaned, and he laughed. "Did you really think I would agree to that?" he asked. "You're with a bunch of men who have sworn to protect you, and, just because we're no longer active duty military, that doesn't mean we're different people."

"Right," she conceded, "but it seems as if the world doesn't appreciate that anymore."

"Maybe not, but, if you had moved to another state, would you be doing this right now?"

"No, of course not." And then she frowned.

And he nodded. "So, why are you doing it in such a panic now?"

"I think she's contacting me in a panic because I'm close by."

"Then she could have gone to a hotel, and she could have asked you to meet her, or even better she could have asked for money to be wired to her."

"She's already asked for money."

"Did she come out and say so in her most recent voice mails?"

She thought about the messages. "No, she did not."

"So, if you were rather desperate for money, what would

you ask for?"

"I would ask for money," she replied.

Burke smiled at her. "I hear what you're saying, and I hope you are registering that too. She didn't ask for that, so that seems a little odd for Silvia, doesn't it?"

Shirley groaned. "You're making it all sound so suspicious now."

"I'm trying to keep you safe," he declared, "and, for that, I just need you to be aware."

"It doesn't feel like being aware," she grumbled, with a dry laugh. "It's looking at my sister in horrible ways."

"Sure," he agreed, "but you already know what she's like. The fact that even you're struggling with what I'm saying is a sure sign that she's already got you hooked."

"She always was good at that," she said suddenly. And she realized just how much her emotions had been causing her to react. "Crap," she muttered, as she stared out the window.

"Crap what?"

"Oh, just memories, memories of her pulling things, you know, … crying wolf on me."

"Has she got a history of that?" he asked, turning to look at her in the dim light.

"Yes and no," she replied, with a headshake. "She's done it a few times, and I always responded to help her out."

"Which is why she's doing it now."

"Sure, but how do you tell if this time isn't a real scenario?"

He shrugged. "We can't, which is why we're going to meet her."

She took a deep breath and let it out. "Thank you."

"As much as I appreciate doing a good job, I don't know

what you're thanking me for right now."

"For giving me a chance to remember who she is on the inside and to not go in there blinded by emotions."

"And that's exactly why I'm doing this," he confirmed. "We're trying to help you. We're willing to help, but we aren't willing to get taken."

"Yes."

Just then they pulled up close to the location she had been given, and he asked, "Why did she choose this location?" He stared out at the park.

"I don't know, but she wanted a public place."

"It's not even six in the morning."

"I know, but don't forget she called me at like four in the afternoon," she reminded him. "What I don't want and what's really been scaring me the whole way in is, ... I'm afraid that when I get here, she's ..."

He turned to face her and asked, "You're afraid she might be dead?"

Tears were in her eyes, as she turned to him. "I guess that's the biggest fear, isn't it?"

"She's definitely triggering fear, ... yes," he agreed. "And, if we thought that were the case, it would be a good thing we are here. No way in hell Frankie will let you go if Silvia is dead," he stated calmly.

"How can you be so calm when she could be ...?" she asked, staring at him.

"Don't think about that now. We don't know that for sure. I'll get out now. You have your phone, and I'll be watching. I'll be close enough to see you," he shared, "but you need to go meet Silvia."

And, with that, he pointed out a vehicle approaching from the far side. He quickly shut off the interior light so it wouldn't go on when he opened the door and stepped out. And, with a last look over at her, he added, "Now you be safe." And, with that, he disappeared.

She got out slowly and walked over to the bench and just sat down, feeling a nervousness she hadn't expected. Even if it was her sister, how much did she really know about her sister these days? Particularly at this stage, when she had pulled such shit on Burke?

Was that just a joke in Silvia's mind?

Or was it something much more serious?

And what the hell could that be?

It was so hard to know who her sister had become. Shirley watched the vehicle park and saw Silvia get out alone, and, with the light going on inside the car, revealing that her sister was truly alone, Shirley felt some of the tension inside her ease. She knew that Burke would see that her sister was alone as well. Shirley sat here and waited.

When Silvia got close enough, Shirley called out in a bitter tone, "What the hell are you playing at?"

Silvia stared at her in surprise.

"You're the one who called me because you were supposedly in trouble."

"I am in trouble," Silvia said, "and it's all your fault."

"I'm not responsible for anything in your world," Shirley declared, "and I have no clue what you're talking about."

"That's only because you're playing at something," Silvia snapped. "Why did you go close that account?"

"What do you mean, *why did I close it*? It was my account, so that's none of your business."

Silvia stared at her. "You don't mean that."

"Of course I do. What are you even talking about? That's my account. It's my money, money that I earned from my job, a paycheck I no longer get because of you, so thank you very much for that."

Silvia stared at her, scrunching up her nose. "What are you talking about?"

"I got fired because of you."

She sat down and looked at her. "Oh."

"Oh? That's all you can say?" Shirley asked, anger bubbling in her. "Shit like that is why I closed that account because I didn't want you turning things around and trying to tell me how I somehow owed you money."

"You do owe me money," she claimed. "I've helped you out tons of times."

She turned and stared at her sister. "What did you just say?"

Even in the dim light, Silvia looked slightly ashamed, and then she rallied quickly. "You know. ... I've helped you. Lots of times ..."

"No, you haven't. I don't know what the hell is going on here or why you even called me out at this godforsaken hour," she snapped, "but I can tell you this. ... It's not about you getting access to my money. Just so we are clear, that's not happening."

Her sister glared at her. "You shouldn't be such a bitch."

"I'm a bitch?" she asked in astonishment.

"Yeah, you are being a basic bitch," Silvia declared, gritting her teeth. "You should share. You should be helping me out."

"Helping you out?" Shirley asked, with a mirthless laugh. "Are you kidding me? All you're doing is running fraud campaigns, and it's only a matter of time before you get picked up by the cops. I am not having anything to do with you and the cons that you're running."

"The cons are a good deal," she stated, and then she stopped. "They're a good deal, until they're not."

"Yeah, they're a good deal, until they're not, and until they're not is a pretty big *not*."

Silvia glared at her. "It's not my fault if people leave all their information lying around for people to steal."

"Seriously? Is that how you got hold of my bank account and my credit cards?"

"Sure, you just left them lying around."

"I left them lying around because it was in my own damn home and I thought I could trust you."

"More the fool," she muttered, followed by a hard laugh.

"Apparently I am a fool. Now … why did you call me here? Because I don't need to be here, and I'm more than ready to head home already."

"Home? Where the hell is home anyway? I went by your place, and it's been completely cleaned out."

"Let's be honest. You tried to get into my bank account. Then you got me kicked out of my apartment, for which you have a key, and you got me fired. Now you've got me out here at six in the morning for something you haven't even explained. You told me that you were in trouble."

"I am in trouble," she snapped, and then she calmed a bit. "And I mean it. I am seriously in trouble."

"Yeah, you really don't look it," Shirley said, realizing that whatever it was that Silvia needed, it had absolutely nothing to do with what she'd said on the phone. "Now I can see that all you wanted to do was cause some drama," Shirley said, "and I really don't need that."

"I don't know what you're talking about," Silvia snapped. "I'm not trying to cause any drama. I need help. I need to get free of Frankie."

Shirley shrugged. "I don't know why I'm supposed to help you. He's your boyfriend, and you told me yourself that you have a good thing going with him. That has zero to do with me."

"I know you don't like him."

"Like him? I don't even know him, but you made a good choice keeping him away from me, although I don't know what it was you were so worried about."

"I always knew that you wanted Burke."

"I always liked Burke," Shirley replied in exasperation. "And what you did to him sucked."

"Whatever. That's so over."

"Is it? You were talking about all the credit cards you had of his."

"Yeah, and they've all been declined now," she grumbled. "I hate it when I have to pay for things."

And she was so pissy about it that Shirley just stared at her. She was at a loss for words for a moment, then shook her head. "I don't even know who you are anymore."

"No, you always knew who I was, but you just didn't want to acknowledge it."

Shirley stood up. "I don't need this. I only came here because you told me that you were desperate and that you needed help."

"I am desperate, and I do need help," she snapped. "I need to get away from Frankie."

"What has that got to do with me?" Shirley asked, staring at her sister.

Silvia glared back. "The least you could do is give me enough money to get free."

"You've got money," Shirley said, with a laugh. "You've got all the money you stole from Burke."

"I spent it all," she snapped. "And why do you keep harping on that? It's not as if he cared."

"What do you mean by that?" she asked. "Does he even know?"

"I don't know, but apparently some cops are looking for me. I'm trying to get free and clear so I can get to another city or something."

"So, just like that, you'll ditch Frankie and go start over with some new guy?"

"Stop being such a prude," Silvia shrieked. "Men are there to be used. That's all there is to it."

"I don't have the same belief system, so no thanks."

"I need money."

Such a hardness filled her sister's tone that Shirley glared at her. "Then go get money, get it from Frankie. You've been stealing from people for however long, so what do you want from me?"

"I want money," she repeated, and her tone changed. "And you'll get me money, or I'll make you."

Shirley snorted. "Oh really? And how do you plan to do that?" It was such a fast maneuver that she had no clue, but all of a sudden a gun appeared in her sister's hand. Shirley stared at it, frowned at her sister, and asked, "Seriously?"

"Yeah, … seriously," she spat. "I keep telling you, and you don't listen, but I need money, and I need to get out of here. Now, sit your ass back down so we can talk about this. You aren't going anywhere until you give me the details and your bank cards."

"I didn't bring them," she stated.

"Then we're going back to your place, and we'll get them."

"And if I say no?" Seeing her cock the gun, Shirley just

stared at Silvia's hand. "You'll shoot me right here, right now?"

"Yeah, I will," she replied. "In case you hadn't figured it out, when I said I need to get loose, I need to get loose. And it's not just because of Frankie. The cops are all over us, so Frankie sent me out here to get money."

"I see." Shirley nodded. "So Frankie sent you here to get the money, and you're once again following along because he said so."

"It's not as if I'll tell him no, will I?" she snapped. "He doesn't take that kindly."

"*Yeah?* I'm not sure I really believe it's him running the show because you're the one pulling the gun on me right now," Shirley pointed out. "So I have no idea what to believe."

"It doesn't matter what you believe," Silvia spat, with an airy wave. "I'm the one with the gun, and you are not leaving until you give me money."

"I haven't got any on me."

"Where's your driver's license?"

She looked around and realized she didn't even have a purse, and she laughed. "I didn't even come with anything," she said. "I thought I was coming to help you, so I came running."

Silvia shook her head. "If you would just be a little more like Dad and me, it wouldn't have been a problem."

"It wouldn't be a problem if you would just get your shit together." Shirley knew she sounded like a broken record.

Silvia snorted. "God, you're so stupid."

Shirley shook her head. "Did you contact Dad and ask him for help?"

"Yeah, ... of course I contacted Dad."

"What did he tell you?"

"What do you think he told me? The damn bastard told me to go get money on my own, that he'd already taught me everything he knew. And, if I'd hooked up with new people and didn't like what I was doing, then it was up to me to go change it," she snapped. "In other words, he told me to F-off."

Shirley considered that and then nodded. "I can see him doing that."

"Of course you can see him doing that," she snorted.

"Did you tell him that Frankie was beating you up?"

"No, I didn't." Then she thought about it and added, "Maybe I should have. I don't know if it would do any good, but it might really piss off Frankie."

"Yeah, … it probably would," Shirley agreed, with a sigh.

Silvia added, "He doesn't take kindly to that either."

"You're playing a long con, and, at some point in time, people are bound to get pissed off at the way you treat them."

"Yeah, … well, right now I need to get out of town, and you're the one who's got what I need. I don't even have gas money."

"Yet you drove here."

"Sure, because I needed money to get here to ask my sister for money because my sister went and closed our bank account."

"*My* bank account," she stated calmly. "It's my money and my account, and no, … you won't convince me that it's anything other than exactly that. *Mine.*"

"From here on out, it's my bank account," Silvia claimed, waving the gun. "Now, let's go to your vehicle, and we'll go to the bank."

"Are you kidding me?" she asked. "Look at the time."

"It doesn't matter, I need money, and you've got it."

"No, I don't, and, even if I did, I wouldn't be giving it to you."

"Have you forgotten who's holding a gun on you?" her sister cried out in astonishment, then she glared. "Why the hell did you all of a sudden grow a spine?"

"Is that what this is to you?" Shirley asked. "Is that how you see me all of a sudden? Like I've grown a spine?" she cried out, looking at her sister.

"Sure, even Pops said you were useless, but that, if I ever needed anything, you would be a good one to come to. Looks as if he was wrong."

"I don't know whether he was wrong or not, but I don't think too many people like being abused and used on a regular basis. So you've played as many cards as I intend to allow you play," Shirley stated, with a smile, "so take a hike."

"I won't take a hike, and I'm not kidding about shooting you."

She stared at her sister. "What do you think Dad would say about that?"

"He'll probably tell me that I should have done it a long time ago. You have no idea, do you? Do you not know just how much he hates you? How much you're just like this … bane on his existence?"

The words hurt, but Shirley refused to let any of it get to her, not when her sister was sitting here, holding a gun on her. "I guess I'm a disappointment to him."

"Yeah, ya think? Jesus, … everything he did to put food on the table and to get us what we needed," she explained, "was for us, and then you turned your back on him."

"You sure didn't need to go to school, find out your friends had shit you didn't, then go home and tell him that he had to get it for you, only for him to steal it off the families of your friends." Shirley stared at her sister, shaking her head. "How the hell is that normal?"

"He couldn't afford it. We knew who had it, so he went and got it. It was simple, and he never took more than I wanted."

"No, but all you did was look at your friends as some secret store, where you could sit and take whatever you wanted."

"Yeah, … well, for the most part that's what they were. They didn't deserve that stuff, certainly not more than I did," she said, staring at her.

"And you wonder why you weren't really friends with anybody."

"I was friends with lots of them," she claimed. "I don't think anybody ever had a clue, or, if they did, they would have done something about it."

"No, they wouldn't have. Dad scared everybody, and he threatened several of them, the families that is. They were all more than happy when we took off," Shirley shared, with another sigh.

"All I wanted was a normal high school experience."

"No, you didn't," Shirley corrected, staring at her sister. "That's the last thing you wanted. You wanted to be the queen bee."

"Whatever. Let's go. Come on. We're taking your vehicle, and we're heading to the bank."

"No, we're not," Shirley argued. "Just shoot me right now."

Silvia stared at her in shock. "What?"

"You heard me." Shirley shrugged. "I am so done playing games with you."

"You don't understand. If I don't show up with that money, I'm the one who'll get shot."

"That may be, but I no longer believe anything you say. You can talk until you're blue in the face, but obviously you're just full of shit, as usual. You're jawing your way through everything, and it makes absolutely no difference to me. I'm done with you."

Her sister stared at her. "I can't believe you're fucking telling me to go. I guess I'll just tell him where you live."

"You don't know where I live," she pointed out calmly. "You don't know anything about me."

"That may be, but you've probably hooked up with bloody Burke. That would so be you. You can't get a man on your own, so you go hook up with my leftovers."

"Too bad you consider him leftovers," Shirley noted in a mocking tone, "because he's a hell of a lot better man than that piece of crap you're sleeping with now."

"Oh God," Silvia muttered, "he's just a man, that's all he is."

"Oh, I hear you, and to you that's all there is, isn't it?"

"Sure, and why not? What do you care?"

"Maybe I don't," Shirley replied, "but I'm not leaving with you. As a matter of fact, I'm going to my car and leaving."

"You're taking that chance?" Silvia asked, as she stood up.

"Yeah, and what chance is that?" Shirley asked.

"That I won't shoot you."

She glared at her sister and left her with a warning. "If you do, make sure that shot is one that counts."

And, with that, she turned and walked to her car.

# CHAPTER 16

BURKE HAD BEEN close enough to listen to the conversation, not surprised when he realized Silvia was literally just trying to get money out of her sister, but, when the gun appeared, pointed at Shirley, his heart froze. To think that Silvia was to the point of using a weapon against her own sister was just shocking. He watched in fear as Shirley moved toward her vehicle. When the shot rang out, he couldn't believe it, but he was already moving quickly, and Silvia was running toward her own vehicle. He knew he could count on the other guys to stop her, but the fact that she'd pulled the trigger was a shock that he might never get over.

He reached Shirley's side, as she collapsed beside her car. "Oh God," he whispered, as he watched the blood well out of her shoulder.

She stared up at him, bewildered. "Was that really my sister?" she asked in tears. "Did she really just shoot me?"

"Yes." He nodded. "It's a flesh wound, so you'll be fine. I only heard one shot."

She nodded at that and then whispered, "Is it bad?"

She didn't say anything more, but such pain filled her words that he wasn't at all sure she was cognizant. "No, it's not bad. It's okay. It'll be just fine." Shock had already set in, and that in itself was a sign of rapid deterioration. He moved her gently into the vehicle, then quickly raced around to the driver's side and headed out at top speed. Jaxon was calling him, and he picked up his cell, while driving. "She's been shot in the shoulder," he told him. "Did you get Silvia?"

"Yeah, we've got her. And the cops are also here."

"Good, hopefully they were close enough to hear and to see what went down."

"I don't know if they heard, but they certainly saw, so that's one good thing."

"Okay, I'm taking Shirley to the hospital, and, if the cops need to talk to her, that's where we'll be." He asked, "Any sign of the boyfriend?"

"No, not yet, but, if he was here, he would have seen us grab her, so he probably took off on his own."

"Yeah, he would have," Burke agreed. "Okay, I'll let you know more from the hospital." And, with that, he ended that call and drove as fast as he could. When he pulled up outside the emergency entrance, he helped her out of her car, then carried her inside, calling out, "Gun shot."

The emergency team sprang into action and quickly had her on a gurney, where they checked her over. He was led outside, where one of the attendants asked him questions about what happened. He gave her a brief explanation, and she just stared at him and then turned and walked back into the emergency room, as if not quite understanding, but then, what the hell? How anybody could not understand this, he didn't know.

As he sat here and waited, he realized he needed to update Timber. Calling Timber was easier, but the explanation was a whole lot worse.

"Silvia shot her, a flesh wound in her shoulder, but I don't know yet how bad it is. None of us expected that," he said, "but Silvia came prepared with the gun."

"Will Shirley be okay?"

"Yes, physically she will, … but it's been a huge shock."

"Yeah, no doubt," Timber noted. "Nothing quite like betrayal to mess with your head, and then when it's a betrayal from somebody really close, … Jesus. She really thought her sister needed help, didn't she?"

"Yes, that's the thing. As far as Shirley was concerned, we were slowing her down in getting to her sister, and her sister could be in major trauma. She was even a little bit afraid we would find her dead. Instead her sister was lying through her teeth and pulled a weapon, trying to get the money she's been after all along."

"Damn it," Timber muttered. "People really suck."

"I know. Anyway I'm here, and I'll check in when I know more. Oh, according to the guys, they grabbed Silvia, and the cops were there, but I don't know anything beyond that."

"I'll contact them and see," Timber replied, "I want to confirm that they've got Silvia in custody and keep her there."

"Yeah, I agree with that."

"But you know what the law is like."

"If they have no money, nobody will bail her out."

"Maybe not, yet Silvia could come up with all kinds of stories to set herself free."

"Like what?" Timber asked. "She shot her sister while she was walking away. It's that *walking away part* that gets me too. Yet Silvia will quite likely say she had to do something to preserve her own life, otherwise this boyfriend would have come in and taken care of her too."

"There's been no sign of him, according to Jaxon," Timber shared.

"No, but I'm not sure I believe that he wasn't around there somewhere."

Timber sighed. "Yeah, … good call. I'm not sure either." And, with that, he rang off.

Burke sat here and waited. When the doctor came out to talk to him, he was smiling and said, "She'll be okay."

"Thank God. I'm sure glad to hear that."

"I don't quite understand what happened, but, because it's a gunshot, we have to call the cops."

"Absolutely," Burke agreed. "My understanding is the authorities already have the shooter in custody, but I don't know that for sure. I just grabbed Shirley and ran."

The doctor added, "This will take a bit of time to heal. Shoulder injuries aren't necessarily fun."

"Right. I know that," Burke acknowledged. "It depends on how bad the wound site is."

"It's not bad, and, if you have a shoulder injury, this is one of the easiest to recover from," he explained, "but it still won't be a walk in the park." Then he saw the prosthetic on Burke's leg, and he nodded. "But I guess you know about that already, don't you?"

"I sure do," he stated calmly. "May I see her?"

"Sure," he agreed, "but she's pretty groggy right now. We're prepping her for surgery."

Burke stared at the doctor in shock.

"The bullet's got to come out."

"Right," he muttered, scrubbing his face. "Don't know why I didn't even consider that."

"Shock," the doc said. "It gets to all of us when it's somebody we care about." With that, he added, "You can stay with her until we take her up."

Burke nodded and he headed to her room, where she

stared up at him, groggy but awake. "Hey," he said, "you're heading up for surgery to get the bullet out."

She winced and nodded. "That sounds like a lot of fun afterward."

"Nope, but apparently, … as far as shoulder injuries go, that is the one you want to have."

"I didn't want to have any," she muttered, her voice thin and pained.

"I'm so sorry, sweetheart." She nodded, and he saw the hot tears in her eyes. He wiped them away. "And I don't know if this news will be a relief or will just be more pain, but the police have picked up your sister."

She blinked and then nodded. "I guess … I just … don't even know what to say."

"Then you don't need to say anything," he suggested. "You've already had more than enough for the day."

She gave a broken laugh. "Isn't that the truth?" she muttered. "How, … how do you recover from this?"

"One day at a time, that's what you do," he suggested, with a smile. "You come back to the Haven, and you recover, … one day at a time."

More tears were in her eyes when she looked at him. "But you don't know that I can go back to the Haven. … Does Timber even want this kind of a nightmare at his place?"

"What nightmare?" Burke asked, with a note of humor. "Silvia's already been picked up."

She frowned at that and then slowly nodded. "Honestly, I'm not so sure that this will be the end of it."

He hesitated, eyed her carefully, and asked, "Do you want to explain that?"

"I'm not sure I can. I just feel as if Frankie is waiting in the background."

"He wasn't seen at the park."

She nodded, but then frowned. "I still feel like he was there."

"Maybe he was," Burke conceded cautiously. "I don't have any way to know."

"No, it's okay," she muttered.

"The surgery will be minor, so keep that in mind," he shared. "Afterward you'll be stiff and sore, but you should come home pretty quickly."

"Now, that would be nice," she whispered, clearly getting drowsier by the minute.

The nurses came in and announced, "We're taking her up now."

"Fine," he said. He stepped back and watched as she was rolled up to surgery on the bed. He followed and was given a space where he could sit and wait. He settled in and sent Timber a text about the surgery. Then he sat down to wait some more.

When the police arrived a little later, he looked up and nodded, as they came over to talk to him. "How is she?" one man asked.

"In surgery, getting the bullet out," he murmured. "Did you pick up the sister?"

He nodded. "We did, and she's spitting mad. She seems to think her sister set her up, and she should have shot to kill her instead of just trying to wound her."

"Did she say why she shot her?"

"She just said she was mad," he replied, looking over at him. "She was just so mad that her sister wouldn't help her. I gather there's quite a history."

"Do you know Detective Martin?" he asked.

"Yeah, I sure do. Why?"

"He's dealing with a fraud case, and this irate woman you've got is the one who's been stealing credit card accounts and using them until they get canceled. Then she turns around and does it again."

"Oh, nice," he muttered, as he picked up his phone. "I'll contact him."

"Please do."

"So, is it all part of the same thing?"

"Yeah, that would make sense." Burke nodded. "Another thing, just before she went under, Shirley insisted that Silvia's boyfriend wasn't likely to have given up on pursuing access to Shirley's assets."

"Boyfriend? Who's that?"

He explained that the only name that he knew him by was Frankie. "That's such a hoodlum kind of name," the cop noted, shaking his head. Just then they were joined by another man. Burke kept on with his explanation as he studied the new arrival. "According to Shirley, Frankie's deadly scary, and that's the only reason she responded when her sister reached out for help. When Silvia said that Frankie was insistent on her getting the money from Shirley, no matter what, she believed her sister. Honestly, I've never seen the guy, but it does make some sense. Do you happen to know Timber and his group?" His gaze encompassed both men.

"Sure do, and Badger and a whole pile of the others," the new arrival confirmed, with a half laugh. "My name is Richard by the way. Detective Richard Martin."

Burke smiled and nodded. "Nice to meet you. I've been staying with Timber for the last several weeks," he explained, "and then we brought Shirley out there after Silvia—the sister you've got in custody—along with her boyfriend Frankie, were pressuring Shirley for money, to the point that she closed her bank account and moved her money elsewhere. The sister raised such a fuss at Shirley's workplace that she lost her job as well."

"Jesus, one hell of a sister, isn't she?"

"No kidding," Burke replied, with a smirk, "and that's another huge problem. Left with no job and no safe place to go, Timber agreed to have Shirley come out to the Haven."

"And that's a hell of a nice place to go to," Richard said, with a nod. "I'm sure that just pissed off her sister more."

"She didn't know where Shirley was, only that she disappeared and had moved her money, afraid that Silvia would end up ripping her off, and, well, … there you have it. And today Silvia baited Shirley out of hiding with a desperate plea for help, which turned out to be a ruse, then ended up shooting her when she wouldn't cooperate, when Shirley was walking away."

"And that's how things escalate in a really ugly way."

"Isn't that the truth?" he muttered. "I just need her to be okay."

"It sounds as if she should be fine, but any surgery, any shooting incident, is just bad news, no matter the situation." Richard straightened and added, "I'll need you to come down to the station."

"Of course." Burke sighed. "It sure would be nice if we could do things digitally."

"You're free to write out a statement and bring it with you," Richard suggested. "In many ways that's not a bad thing. I can build on that as soon as I get it."

"Maybe I will," he replied. "I've got nothing better to do right now."

After setting up a meeting time, he said goodbye to Detective Martin. As soon as he was alone again, Burke brought out his phone, opened the notepad, and painfully started to describe what happened. As soon as he had everything down as best as he could, he sent it off to the detective. He ended up closing his eyes and just resting while he waited and waited and waited. It seemed like forever, then suddenly the doctor stood in front of him.

He smiled and noted, "Glad you caught some rest."

"Nothing like a shock to get your adrenaline going. Then as soon as it stops ..."

The doctor smiled and nodded. "As soon as it stops, it drops," he interjected. "I hear you. Anyway, she is out of surgery. She'll be fine, and everything went well. We've got the bullet, which will go to the police. We'll keep her overnight, and then we'll see how she's doing tomorrow."

"Good enough," Burke said, with a sigh. "Glad to know everything went well."

"Of course." He smiled. "It is highly recommended that she stays overnight." Then he frowned and asked, "Does she have insurance?'

He frowned at him. "I don't really know. ... I suppose it matters though, doesn't it?"

"No, not necessarily. Even if she's not working, she might still have medical insurance. And, if she just lost her job, it's usually still good for thirty days afterward."

"That's good to know. I guess we'll find out from her when she wakes up, won't we?"

The doctor nodded, and he left Burke sitting here, worried about something so simple as insurance. Yet it was a huge thing for so many people, and it should be because, without it, people were left in really rough straits.

As soon as they moved her from recovery to a private room, he was allowed to be with her. He sat at her side and just waited as she slept. She woke up a couple hours later, and it was almost noon.

He smiled as she surfaced, and he asked, "Hey, how are you doing?"

She looked at him and shuddered. "Not exactly what I thought my morning would be like," she admitted, "but I guess you were right. I shouldn't have gone."

His eyebrows shot up, and he shook his head. "No, … absolutely not. That's not how this goes," he said, with a smile. "We don't think that anybody is right or wrong in an instance like this. You had to go see if your sister was in trouble, and we all understood that."

"And yet, because of her, now I'm in trouble," she replied.

"I hate to ask this, but they did want to know if you had insurance."

"I do," she said, waving her good arm, "but I forgot to bring my purse with me. It's back at Timber's place. I was so spun up and worried about Silvia that I left without it. That's probably one of the reasons Silvia was so frustrated that she ended up shooting me. She was really pissed off."

"Possibly but, … if she has any money, she should pay for this."

"Any money she has is probably from your credit cards."

He winced at that. "And I would pay for it, except I'm not even sure what kind of money we're talking about."

She smiled and added, "Not necessary. I do have insurance from my old job." She sighed. "The insurance from that is still good. Plus, I did take out a private policy after leaving the project management world, so I should be okay."

"That's good to know," he said. "I didn't want to stress you out with that and have you worrying about money too."

"No, it's not a problem," she muttered. "Everybody has to deal with insurance, and thankfully I could afford to take care of it."

He smiled and nodded. "That was really smart of you. As soon as you're feeling better, we can get you home."

"Tonight?" she asked hopefully but frowned at his head-shake. "Do I have a choice?"

"Nope," he said, with half a laugh. "Do you want me to get you anything?"

"You might as well go home," she suggested. "I'll probably just fall asleep." And, with that, she was already yawning.

The nurse came in, hearing her say that. "Sleep is exactly what you need." She turned and looked at him. "You can stay here, but the best thing for her is to let her nod off."

"Right," he replied, and, even as they watched, Shirley fell asleep in front of them. "I'm hoping she can come home soon."

"As soon as the doctor releases her, but not before," the nurse said, with a smile. "I understand she's been shot, so she is still in shock, and all kinds of stuff are going on. So we need her strong enough to ensure she doesn't have anything in there go south. So, if you see something, anything at all, we can't play around with this. We'll talk about tomorrow when it comes and when we see how she is," she explained. "You should go do something you need to do, and, if you want to come back tonight, that's fine. Maybe she'll be more awake, but, then again, she might be asleep."

"Right, ... and I'll have no way of knowing that either."

"You can call," she suggested. "You absolutely can call."

"Okay, maybe I'll do that." With that, he kissed Shirley

on the cheek, and, with one final look at her, he smiled at the nurse and added, "Hopefully tomorrow."

"I would think so. It's not a big injury after all, and, with any luck"—she gave him a smile—"it'll be something she'll recover from very quickly."

Burke had to be happy with that.

# CHAPTER 17

S HIRLEY WOKE LATER that afternoon, the pain absolutely excruciating. The nurses were there almost immediately and smiled at her and asked, "How are you feeling?"

"Probably as you would expect," she muttered. "Kind of like somebody just put a hot burning poker through my shoulder."

"Yeah, that sounds about right." She was quickly checked over, and her pain meds were delivered.

As soon as that happened, she looked around. "Was anybody here?" Shirley asked hopefully.

"If you're looking for the man who has been at your side the whole time, we sent him home while you got a chance to rest, as he needed to do some other things," she shared. "Or maybe we told him to go get other things done."

"Right," she said, with a sigh. "That sounds like Burke."

"He's really cute."

She nodded. "Of course, but he doesn't think so."

"That always makes for the best kind though," the nurse said, with a laugh.

She smiled at that. "You're right there," she muttered, checking her name tag. *Willow.*

"Anyway, he's not here right now," Willow confirmed, "but he's been here for the most part. He settled down after you were safely out of surgery."

"Okay, that's good to know."

"He was very attentive, so you're a very lucky lady."

She looked over at her, half smiled, and let the world start to fade away again as the pain meds kicked in. She woke up again, fell back asleep, and then woke up one more time, starting to feel a little bit better. It was dark out, but she had lost all sense of time. When the nurse came in, Shirley asked, "What time is it?"

"It's nine o'clock," she replied. "You've been sleeping pretty heavily most of the day."

"I do feel better now though. I guess there's no chance of a shower yet, *huh*?"

"Nope, not a chance," she stated cheerfully, "but maybe tomorrow morning."

"That would be nice," she muttered.

"And we do understand how it feels," she noted, "but we want to give you the best chance to heal as we can."

"That makes sense."

"Are you expecting company tonight?"

"I don't know whether Burke will come back or not," she said, with a yawn. "There are a lot of animals to look after."

"He has called a couple times today to see if you were awake."

"Ah." She smiled. "That is nice to know."

"He seemed very concerned about you."

She nodded. Just that news alone made her feel so much better. She knew that Burke didn't want to go back into that whole family thing again, but the ache in her heart would never heal, knowing that he had chosen her sister over her, and then her sister had turned around and had treated him so badly.

When the nurse came in shortly after that, she held out a phone. "It's Burke," Willow announced, with a smile.

She reached out with her good arm, wincing as she shifted a little too much.

Willow handed it to her with a warning. "Yeah, you'll have to make smaller movements for a while," she suggested, with a smile.

"You're not kidding," she muttered. She cheerfully answered the phone. "Hey, Burke. I'm fine."

"Are you sure?" he asked, his tone heavy and still worried.

"I'm a whole lot better than I was, so thank you very much for getting me to the hospital."

"Right," he said, with a note of humor. "Things blew up really quick."

"I'm not even sure what that was," she replied, trying not to move. "I never ever would have thought Silvia would shoot me."

"She also shot you in the back."

"Yeah, … that says an awful lot too, doesn't it?" she asked, with a sigh.

"I'm on my way back into town," he told her. "I was just checking to see if you were awake and up for a visit."

"I would absolutely love a visit," she said warmly.

"Good, and you should know that I told the nurse we were engaged, so they would let me stay and visit with you."

Her heart slammed against her chest at that news. "What?" she asked in confusion.

"They only allow family."

"Oh, right. I guess that makes sense."

"And, by the way, everybody here sends you their best and are hoping you'll recover quickly."

"I'm sure—except for Timber, who's probably hoping I'm dying, so he doesn't have to face the whiteboards."

He burst out laughing at that. "I'm pretty sure he wants you to get your ass back here so he does everything right because that whiteboard scares the crap out of him."

She smiled. "I appreciate the sense of humor."

"I'll be there in about twenty minutes. So hang tight. Then we can talk." With that, he disconnected.

She relaxed back into the bed and closed her eyes. Twenty minutes was nothing, and she was feeling much better than she had all day. She shifted around a bit, then realized she needed to go to the bathroom. One of the other nurses came in and made sure she was able to get there on her own, waiting outside the door to confirm she was okay. As she made her way out of the bathroom and gingerly climbed back into bed, the nurse added, "It sounds as if your friend should be here soon."

"Yes," she confirmed, with a bright smile.

When the nurse disappeared, Shirley sank back. Then, hearing a noise at the door, she shifted to face him, a bright smile on her face, then froze because it wasn't Burke. It was Frankie.

He looked at her and glared.

"Hello, Frankie," she said.

"What the hell is going on here?"

She stared at him. "You tell me. Apparently you convinced Silvia to shoot me."

He blinked several times and repeated, "She shot you?"

"Yeah, she shot me," Shirley stated bitterly. "How did you find out I was here?"

"She called me from jail."

"I'm not surprised."

"I can't imagine your sister in jail."

"Honestly, neither can I."

"So, you'll need to help her," he noted calmly. "That's what family does."

She stared at him, then snorted. "Family does help family, but you know what family doesn't do?" she asked, almost bursting with anger. "Family doesn't shoot each other."

He looked at her and said, "I don't believe she shot you."

"Of course you don't," she noted, with a wave of her hand. "Yet it was witnessed by quite a few people."

"*Right*, according to you."

She smiled. "Have you talked to the cops?"

"Nope, I don't do cops."

"Ah, must be a nice option, considering."

"Yeah, it is a nice option."

"That's lucky for you, but Silvia's in jail. She was picked up for this little shooting, right on the scene."

He hesitated and asked, "Did she really do it?"

"Yes, she really did it," she spat, glaring at him. "She said you were the reason, that she was scared of you and needed to disappear and get free of you. The fact that I didn't have any money for her meant she would be in trouble with you, and, when I walked away from her, she shot me in the back."

That news seemed to really surprise him. "She shot you in the back?"

"Yes, she shot me in the back," she repeated, glaring at him.

He stared off in the distance. "That's interesting."

"Why?"

"I didn't think she had it in her," he muttered, with half a smile.

"I'm sure you're delighted to know who she is on the inside."

"It's always nice to know. I can't really say much about it because I'm not sure I believe you," he shared, with a shrug, "but I guess I'll need to have a talk with her."

"You can probably call her in jail. … I don't know."

"She already called me," he noted, "but I didn't accept it."

She frowned at him. "Okay, and why is that?"

"If she's going down, I'm not going with her," he declared calmly. "That's not part of the deal. She had no reason to shoot you, I gather it was …" He stopped and just shook his head. "I can't really see it. I think it must have been out of temper."

Shirley shrugged at that.

"Now that I can see, but I'm still not going down with her because, once they figure out all the shit I've done," he explained, "I'll never see daylight again. Whereas your sister, while I don't know what they'll do about this, it's her first offense."

"Except for all the fraud."

"Except for the fraud."

"Which they do know about, so I don't know that she'll get away very easily."

He studied her for a long moment. "It only became a problem when she decided to go after somebody she knew, and, the minute you do that, all bets are off."

She stared at him, not sure what he was saying, but something about the look in his eyes she didn't like. "When you say she was going after—"

"Yeah," he interrupted. "You take credit cards from strangers, not from people you know. That adds an element of personal revenge that never works in this industry."

"If you say so," she muttered, wishing he would just go away.

He glanced around a couple times and said, "I heard the nurse say you were expecting somebody."

"Yes," she replied, then realized the last thing she wanted was for Frankie to see Burke. "Why?"

"I told them you were expecting me, and she seemed to smile, like it was perfect."

"Of course," she muttered, sagging back warily. "And why are you here?"

"Just trying to confirm what stunt your sister had pulled to land herself in jail."

"I'm not in the hospital for nothing."

"That just means that she and I are done," he said, with a nod. "Which is really too bad because it was the kind of a con that worked, and she was really good at that part."

Shirley winced. "Yeah, apparently she was, but how is that good though?"

"It was good for me, not so good for her," he clarified, with a chuckle, "but it's not my problem now. You should have just given her the money." With that, he picked up the backpack he had on the floor beside him. She hadn't even noticed it. "I just have one more thing to take care of."

"What's that?" she asked, frowning.

He looked at her, smiled, then lifted a small handgun, pointing it right at her. "You."

She shuddered.

"I highly suspect that to save her own ass, she'll open up about all kinds of things," he added. "She can make up whatever story she wants. She can't prove any of it, but you, on the other hand, if you back up some of it or give them any information, it'll just lend weight to it."

She looked at him with a puzzled expression, a sense of dread creeping up her spine.

He shrugged. "That is something I just can't have. You may have survived her attack, but you won't survive mine."

And, with that, he fired.

# CHAPTER 18

BURKE WALKED INTO the hospital, smiled at the woman at the reception desk, then headed up to Shirley's room. He passed one of the nurses who just smiled at him but kept on going, realizing that it was visiting hours, or at least after visiting hours, so only friends and family would be allowed. He'd already covered that, at least he hoped he had, and didn't want any nurse to be worrying about something so simple. It shouldn't be an issue, although he understood why the hospital had to have such rules as part of their system. It made sense to restrict the number of people who came and went, but he wasn't prepared to let Shirley be all alone in there, not if he could do something about it.

As he neared Shirley's hospital room, one of the nurses from behind him called out, "Who are you visiting, sir?"

"Shirley."

"Shirley, … the one with the gunshot wound?" she asked in confusion.

"Yes," he said, stopping and recognizing her from before. "That's all right, isn't it?" he asked, as he continued to walk backward.

She frowned. "Yes, … but I thought her fiancé was already here."

He stared at her. "What? No. … That would be me."

"Somebody came by to see her earlier, and I noticed he

was directed to her room."

"Don't you guys keep an eye on things like that, especially with a gunshot victim?" His footsteps automatically picked up, moving faster and faster.

She just shrugged and replied, "It depends on who they are."

He wasn't even sure what that meant, and she probably wasn't sure either, but, as he raced forward, he realized that meant Shirley had a visitor who was most likely somebody she didn't want to see.

He slowed as he approached her hospital room door from the side. He heard voices, not voices that gave him any sense of calm. A man spoke to her, his tone suddenly turning hard, even as Burke approached the doorway. He stepped inside just as the man lifted his hand. With shock he saw a handgun pointed directly at Shirley, and she cried out, even as the gun fired, but she rolled to the side, and Burke hit the gunman a split second later. Both men went tumbling down, but Frankie came back up in a fighter's stance. Burke rolled out, kicking the gun from his hand. Frankie rolled off to the side, grabbing for the gun, as Burke was on his feet and heading toward the newest threat on her life.

As Frankie bounced back to his feet, the gun now turned in Burke's direction, he heard Shirley call out in shock, but Burke was already moving, trying to nullify the threat, not pointed right at him now. It was all he could do to get out of the way in time, but he did, as the gun went off a second time, shooting harmlessly into the floor. He knew that would bring security running, or at least he hoped so.

It was the wrong time of night for very many people to be here, but there should at least be somebody interested in keeping people safe. Burke wasn't sure what the hell was going on, but he was looking at the man who was on his feet yet again, with the gun in hand and a smile on his face.

"Well, dang, I guess you're the missing Burke, aren't you?"

Burke stared at him and then glared. "Are you Frankie, by any chance?"

The other man nodded. "Yeah, that would be me," he confirmed, with a cheerful smile. "Too bad you showed up. I didn't have anything against you, not personally at least, not like somebody else we know, but that's just too damn bad for you." Then he laughed, a wolfish laugh, but then the smile fell away. "I'm just trying to get the hell out of here, so you can either get out of my way or you can take the next bullet."

Burke just smiled at him and said, "How about neither?" With that, he lunged forward, ferociously kicking the handgun free with his prosthetic, while Frankie jumped, swearing at him.

"Ain't no fucking way," Frankie yelled, kicking back at Burke. "I'm not staying in this hick town and paying the price for that bitch," he muttered. "She's sheer poison."

"She's the poison you hooked up with," Burke stated calmly, as the two circled each other.

"And that's supposed to mean what?" he asked. "You were there before me."

"Yeah, and so were a lot of other guys," Burke noted. "That's just how she rolls."

"And yet she holds it all against you."

"I'm the one who walked away from her, and apparently I'm not allowed to do that in her book."

"She's causing me all kinds of trouble now," Frankie shared, "so I'm not sticking around."

"Of course not," Burke noted, with half a smile. "Nobody who's about to lose everything is planning on sticking around."

"I'm not losing shit," he declared, glaring at him. "She's just plain trouble, and she likes this life a little too much."

"Yeah, I noticed," Burke said. "It seems as if maybe you do too."

"No," he argued. "I'm all about making smart decisions, and she is not a smart decision."

"Too bad you didn't see that a little sooner."

"You're not kidding," he admitted. "I should have seen it, and I should have run for the hills, but it was fun while it lasted. Until I realized just how much she had against you, but I'm still not exactly sure why."

"Neither am I," Burke replied. "All I can tell you is that she doesn't like being the one left behind."

"Yeah, I know that," he acknowledged, with a smile. "I told her, if she came back for more revenge on you, I was walking. She didn't believe me, so guess what? I'm walking."

"Well. … you'll try to walk, but you came in here with a handgun, intending to kill an innocent woman, and why? Hasn't Shirley already been through enough?"

"Maybe, but that's not my problem. It's all about self-preservation at this point, and you know that too."

"Maybe," Burke conceded, "but that would also mean you must take out Silvia."

"I considered it. I really did." He laughed. "The trouble is, she's under lock and key. So anything she says right now isn't likely to go anywhere. It'll be her word against mine, and, since I won't be around, she'll have all kinds of tales to tell, but she's not exactly in a position of good standing with the cops herself," he pointed out. "So I doubt they'll believe very much of what she says. It'll all just come across as her being sour and looking for a scapegoat to cover her own crimes," he stated, with a smile. "Not my problem."

Burke looked at him and tilted his head. "That might have worked if you had left town, but you didn't. You came after Shirley instead."

"Oh, and I suppose you won't let me pull that off, right?" he asked in a mocking tone.

Burke smiled at him and shook his head. "No, I won't. She's been to shit and back already and doesn't need any more of that from you guys."

"Oh, as if you care," he said in a mocking tone.

"Maybe to you it's nothing," Burke noted, "but Shirley and I have both suffered from that crazy sister of hers, and I'm pretty well done with that."

"Yeah, anybody who sticks around Silvia is looking to get in trouble," he noted. "I don't know where she's going next, but you might want to confirm it's not in your direction."

"Wasn't planning on it," Burke stated. "I've already got quite a bit of evidence against her."

He shrugged. "Don't really care if you do or you don't. Just keep yourself away from me, and we'll get along fine. But if you don't ..." He turned and caught a glance of the gun on the floor beside him.

Burke repeated, "And if I don't?"

As Frankie took a step toward his weapon, Burke immediately shifted his weight.

"Look, hero. I'm taking that gun, and I'm going. If you want to stop me, you can try, but it won't go well for you."

"Oh, I'll stop you," Burke vowed, with a smile. "It won't be a case of *trying*. It's about time for you to pay the piper, along with your girlfriend."

"I didn't do nothing to you," Frankie snapped. "Just let me leave, and it's all good."

"Except that you just tried to take out Shirley," he pointed out, glaring at Frankie. "The fact that you came after her here means you'll come back later and try again."

Frankie frowned and then shrugged. "No, that's just a bad deal for me now."

"It's more than a bad deal," Burke murmured. "You can't be trusted."

"That's part of the problem now because you don't know what you can do and what you can't do," he said, with a cocky smile, "and I'm not about to sit here and let you ruin the rest of my life. I already went through hell with that bitch, and I'm done wasting time and energy on the bitch's sister, even if she does have some money."

But even as he said that, he took a dive toward the gun on the floor. As soon as he bent down, Burke sent him a hard high kick, hitting him square in the jaw and sending him flying backward, where he dropped and thankfully stayed.

A slow clapping sound came from the doorway.

Startled, Burke turned to see Detective Martin and one of the doctors standing there. Burke glared at him and asked, "What kind of security are you running in this place anyway?"

"I wasn't planning on running any security," the doctor replied, frowning at him. "Honestly, I wasn't thinking that we needed any." He looked down at the gunman and asked, "Who the hell is he?"

Burke looked over at Detective Martin and pointed. "That's your suspect, Frankie."

"Not Frankie," he countered, with a chuckle. "His name is François," he stated, with an exaggerated accent. "And he is wanted on all kinds of charges." Richard kicked the gun farther away, then pulled out his own weapon and checked to see if Frankie was out. "He won't be going anywhere for a while," he declared, with a delighted smile. "And this is a collar I am more than happy to accept your help with."

"Yeah, well, it would have been nice if you'd been here a little sooner."

"I was here a little sooner," he declared, with a smug look on his face. "But since you were handling it so well, and getting information out of him in the process, I didn't want to ruin it."

From the bed, Shirley whispered, "Is it over?"

The doctor immediately walked closer. "Are you okay?"

"I don't know if I am or not," she said. "Honest to God, I really just want to get the hell out of here and get back to the Haven, where I'm safe."

"Lucky you for having a spot at the Haven," Detective Martin said, looking over at Burke now. "Timber's got quite a place there."

She looked at him in surprise. "Do you know Timber?"

"I do, and we go way back. I was out there with him dealing with some trouble that happened a couple months or so ago," he replied, with a small smile. "And, if you've got a way of staying out there long enough to get yourself healed and to get your life together, take it."

"I was hoping I could stay for a little bit longer," she replied, "but I couldn't risk bringing this trouble down on their shoulders."

"You can bring all the trouble down on their shoulders that you need to," Richard stated, with a laugh. "I've got to tell you, they're well prepared to take on all that trouble and to ensure none of it comes back to anybody."

"And is that good or bad?" she asked on a sigh.

"It's good, and those are all damn good people," he added, with a big grin. He looked over at Burke. "You tell Timber that, as far as I'm concerned, we're free and clear on this one."

"That would be good," Burke replied. "She needs a place to rest up before any more shit hits the fan."

"I still need a statement."

Burke nodded. "A statement you can have."

"Are you sure about that?" she asked, as she looked from one to the other. "Honest to God, I'm feeling a little bit on the rough side for giving statements."

"It'll be more from him this time, but we'll take your statement too," Richard replied. He walked closer, grinned at her, and said, "If you're over at the Haven, I'll see you around. I go up there quite a bit."

"That's nice to know," she replied, studying him. "I hadn't realized Timber had good friends in the area."

"He has a lot of good friends," he confirmed, "and he's a really good friend to have."

She nodded. "He's been a huge help, letting me stay there."

Then he stopped and stared at her. "Oh my gosh, are you the one who's been tormenting him with the whiteboards?" She flushed, and Richard started to laugh. "Oh, I am so happy to send you back there. Anybody who can get that guy organized …"

"He was doing pretty well before I got there," she protested. "It's just, … he's got so many projects on the go that things were starting to slip between the cracks."

"Oh, yeah. That's a great way to put it." And he chuckled, looked down at the man still unconscious on the ground, and whistled. "Dang good thing you're not out there kicking us around," he shared, turning to look at Burke.

Burke smiled and explained, "The prosthetic is one of Kat's, and it delivers one hell of a kick."

Richard looked at it with admiration. "You guys could use a few more like that too, you know?"

"I know," Burke agreed, "and we're working on it. Just need to get through insurance, and sometimes that's a little easier said than done."

"I hear you there," Richard noted. "Anyway, I'll take this guy downtown. Before you head back tomorrow, I need you to stop in for statements." He stopped, looked at both of them. "Agreed?"

Shirley nodded. "Yes, … agreed."

He looked back over at Burke, who nodded and replied, "Will do."

"She stays here overnight though," the doctor added firmly.

"That's fine," Burke acknowledged, "but I'm not leaving her side."

"Yeah, I figured as much. I'll have a cot brought it."

With a sigh, the doctor headed off, and, in a surprise move, Richard grabbed Frankie, gave him a hard shake, and said, "Get your ass on your feet."

Now that he was handcuffed and wouldn't go far, Frankie opened one eye, saw who it was, and glared at him. "No fucking way did I get dropped by an amputee," he snapped.

"But you did, you absolutely did." Richard laughed.

"Plus, your girlfriend is waiting for you in jail."

"She ain't my girlfriend," he snapped.

"That's not what she says."

"I don't care what she says," Frankie yelled. "That woman is a nightmare. And to do that to her sister? Shooting her in the back? None of that has anything to do me."

"That's not what she's saying."

"Yeah, you want to stay a long way away from her. If I had the smarts, I would have run when I had the chance. I just wasn't sure about this one," he shared, as he turned and glared at Shirley, still lying in the hospital bed.

She just glared right back at him. "Yeah, I'm still alive. And I'll still be alive whenever you get out of prison again," she added. "So, don't be thinking any more shit about coming after me."

"I wasn't," he said. "I just wanted to get the hell out of town and to get away from all of you. You are all psychos, every freaking one of you. Do you have any idea what their dad's like?" He twisted to ask Richard.

"No, but if you want to tell me about it, feel free."

"Yeah, well, he's one of the worst."

# CHAPTER 19

S HIRLEY WATCHED AS Frankie walked out, still mumbling, trying to save his ass with the detective.

Then Burke walked over, standing beside her. He picked up her hand and held it gently. "Hey. How are you doing?"

She smiled. "Honest to God, … I'm not really sure, but I don't want to go through that again. Yet it's a hell of a relief to know that we are done with both of them."

"He wasn't that bad," Burke teased, with a big grin.

She groaned. "Maybe to you he's not that bad, but when that gun went off …"

The smile immediately fell from his face, and he nodded. "I hear you there," he murmured. "I'm so sorry."

She looked over at him and smiled. "You have no idea how much I appreciate everything you've done for me."

He frowned at her. "Oh no, no, no," he muttered. "That sounds like a goodbye."

She frowned. "It's not so much a goodbye as much as a, … *Hey, I really appreciate what you did for me,*" she teased.

"Ah, well, that is one thing, but that sound of a goodbye is a completely different thing."

She looked at him and admitted, "I wasn't sure if you even wanted to say hello after this."

"Of course I do," he stated. "I meant what I said earlier."

"You mean when you said you made the mistake of going out with the wrong sister?"

"Yeah, I did mean that."

She snorted. "You have no idea how many times my sister told me the exact same thing."

"That was a mistake I made, but it's not a mistake I'm willing to keep making."

She frowned. "I'm not sure about that."

"Absolutely no reason for either of us to think of Silvia at all."

"Are you sure?"

"Absolutely sure. Besides, the guys already really love you."

"Oh, so the guys really love me, so I'm safe to go back there. Is that it?" she asked, with smile.

"Believe me, once they found out what happened, all kinds of hell was happening out there, so if you're not coming back to the Haven, I'll be in deep shit."

"You will?"

"Yes, because they'll all think it will be because you don't want to come back with me."

"Is that the condition to coming back?" she asked.

"No," he said instantaneously, "absolutely not. No strings attached."

She looked up at him, now with her lips twitching, and asked, "Are you sure?"

"I am," he replied, "but if you do want to spend time together—"

"I do," she stated instantly.

His face split in a wide grin. "I was hoping you would say that. I just, … I wasn't sure."

"Yeah, well, neither am I," she admitted, a bit flushed. "Not really. It's a weird scenario. Looks as if I'll have to stay in town to deal with my sister, after all."

"No, she'll be in jail, and then you'll be free, though there will probably be a trial."

"Yeah, because she won't confess to anything," she guessed, with a sigh. "She'll make sure my life is as difficult as it can possibly be."

"That's her right, but that doesn't mean it'll go easy on her, even if she does. Especially as Frankie is singing to save his soul. Also the credit cards are wiping out the debt as this is now part of a criminal investigation and they know it wasn't you using up the cards."

"That's huge! I suppose I hadn't really considered that part," she noted. "I wasn't really even thinking, to be honest. I was more concerned about trying to stay alive." She looked down at the sheet around her. "They mentioned they would send you a cot, didn't they?"

"They did and they will."

Just then the door opened and an orderly walked in with a cot. He asked, "Is this for you?"

He nodded. "Yep, that's for me."

"Good enough. I heard some nightmare was going on here a little while ago."

"Yeah, there sure was," Burke confirmed. "We had a shooting in here."

The orderly looked at him shock. "Seriously?"

"Yeah, seriously, that's why I'm staying here for the night."

"Well." He looked over, saw Shirley, and smiled. "Honest to God, man, you don't need an excuse. She's amazing, and, hey, I would be staying here too if I could." And, with a wink, he turned and left them alone.

"Did he just say that?" Shirley asked in astonishment.

"Yeah, he did," Burke replied with a grin. "Seems as if you have a fan."

"That would be a first."

He shook his head. "No, it wouldn't, and we need to get rid of all that leftover family BS too."

"Yeah, I'm happy to have that go," she admitted. "It'll just take a bit of time."

"It may, and then it may not," he pointed out. "The fact that you don't know how beautiful you are, both inside and out, is a shame, but it is to my benefit. I'll be more than happy to show you how much everybody loves you."

She looked over at him, tears in her eyes.

"Hey, hey, no tears, please."

She snorted. "As if I'll just stop because you say so."

"Of course you will," he teased, with a big grin. "I know it's been one hell of a day."

"No, it's been a hell of a few days," she corrected. "Ever since I realized what was happening and knew I had to make some major decisions."

"Ah, but you made them," he noted, "and you made the right ones, so that's what counts."

She smiled. "I hope so. The last thing I want is to find out that I messed up in some other way."

"That's just your father speaking."

"Oh God, it is so my father speaking," she admitted, with a sigh. "You don't even realize."

"Now that stage of your life is over."

There was such firmness in his tone that she wanted to believe him, was sorely tempted to believe him, but knew it would take time before she got to that point. Also that it wouldn't happen so quickly. He looked at her as if he knew what she was thinking.

"Yeah, it'll take a little time," he stated, "but you're almost there, and that is just as important."

She looked over at him and shook her head. "I don't even know how you could possibly understand what I was thinking."

"If you understood what I was thinking, this would be a whole different conversation," he stated, then waggled his eyebrows at her.

She flushed bright red and then laughed. "That is good news," she murmured, as she opened her good arm, wincing at the pain of moving the other one. "Damn, that'll take a bit."

"It sure will," he said, with a bright smile. "That's what happens when you try to be a hero."

"I wasn't being a hero."

"Yes, you were," he argued. "You were trying to reach out and to help your sister."

She frowned and then nodded reluctantly. "But it wasn't, … it's not as if I wanted to be a hero."

"I know," he said, "but that is who you are, and that is something you'll just have to accept."

She smiled up at him, "Only if you do too."

"Oh no, no, no, no,"

"Oh yes, yes, yes, yes," she replied. He glared at her, and she burst out laughing. "If I do, you do."

He sighed. "Okay, fine, I will consider it."

"Done."

And, with that, he leaned over and gave her a gentle hug, avoiding her bandaged shoulder. "Now, would you get yourself back to sleep so we can leave this place tomorrow?"

"Now that is well worth trying."

He helped her shuffle into a better position in the hospital bed, pulled up the covers, then gave her a gentle kiss on the forehead. "Get some sleep, please. I do want to get out of here as soon as possible."

"Done," she murmured, "but it might take me at least until tomorrow."

"You'll get until tomorrow," he said. "You'll get as long as you need. Just rest."

# CHAPTER 20

SHIRLEY WOKE THE next morning and stretched, wincing, stopping the movement almost immediately on the one side, but overall she felt a whole lot better. She had to admit that she felt quite decent. She knew that it would be a problem to not do too much, particularly when she got back to the Haven, but it was something that she was really looking forward to. She rolled over and realized that Burke wasn't even here.

Whether he had left in the night, she didn't know, but he was long gone. She frowned at that, and then the door opened almost immediately, as he stepped in, carrying coffee.

He handed her one cup and said, "I figured that this might go down pretty well."

"How did you know I would be awake?"

"You started to snuffle a little bit ago," he shared, with smile. "So I headed out to get you some coffee to wake up to."

She laughed in appreciation. "Now this is something I could get used to."

"I don't think you've been used to anybody looking after you in a very long time."

She frowned, then nodded. "I don't think that's an experience I've ever had."

"Right, well, … that's just one more thing to fix."

"Oh, and you'll be chief fixer, will you?" she teased.

"Absolutely," he agreed, with a big grin. "Besides, I wouldn't want anybody else to do the job." He handed her the coffee.

She sniffed the rich aroma and smiled. "How is it that anything resembling coffee is just the perfect answer after a long day?"

"And is this a long day?" he asked, looking at her in astonishment. "Personally I figured it wasn't even the start of a day."

"No, you're right there, but that's okay. It feels as if it has the makings of a long day already."

He laughed and added, "You're going home today, so maybe that'll help."

"That'll help a lot," she murmured. "However, I'll need to get cleared by the doctor first."

"Yeah, you will, and then it's home time."

While she sipped the coffee, the nurses came around, did their check of her vitals at each shift change, and then shared, "The doctor will be in before long."

As soon as they left, Burke suggested, "I'll go pick up the groceries, then I'll come back and pick you up too."

And that's what they did. By the time he returned, she had been released and was just maneuvering back into her clothes. As she stood here, he stepped in just as she was done. He frowned at her and shook his head. "Sorry, I didn't think to bring you anything clean."

"That's okay. I can get changed when we get back."

"Good enough." He pushed her in a wheelchair back to the vehicle, which was already fully loaded.

She smiled. "I guess this is just a normal grocery load for Timber, isn't it?"

"It is when you constantly need supplies to keep the new construction going. Plus, he's got a lot of mouths to feed out there."

"Right. It seems like such a long time ago, and yet it was only yesterday."

"Yes," he agreed, giving her a bright smile. "It was both a long time ago and just yesterday. Somehow, it seems as if a lifetime since then."

"Right, because a lot of things transpired. Did I ever thank you for coming into town with me, even when I was so determined that you shouldn't?"

He laughed. "Yeah, well, … we wouldn't let you go alone," he stated. "So you would either go, knowing we were there, or you would go, thinking you were alone, but either way we would be there."

She smiled, then bent closer and whispered, "Thank you."

"You still got shot, so I can't say that we did a great job."

"Oh my, that's not the point. The point is that you cared enough to even think about it."

He shook his head. "I wouldn't mind trashing that father of yours for the treatment you received at his hands."

"Ah, that's an old story," she muttered. "I really don't have any intention of going back there."

"Good," he agreed, "because I don't really want anything to do with him either."

"It's not as if we'll have anything to do with either of them. Plus, they won't want anything to do with us after this."

"Perfect," he muttered. Then he looked over at her as he drove through town, heading back toward the Haven, and in a low voice he asked, "So, I guess that means we can have a small wedding, *huh?*"

She gasped in shock. "What did you say?"

He burst out laughing. "Was that a little too much, a little too fast?"

She stared at him. "I know you're joking because you don't even know me."

"But I do know you," he countered. "I know everything that counts, and, besides, we were great friends before."

"We were," she agreed, "and that's one of the reasons I felt so terrible when I realized she was stealing from you."

"We'll park that and not worry about it anymore," he said, "because that isn't today's issue."

"Maybe not, but it still feels very much like something I should have known about."

"And what could you have possibly done?" he asked. "You did everything you could, as soon as you found out."

"Do we still have to go see the detective?"

He froze, swore, and muttered, "Yeah, we do." He quickly changed directions, then added, "I forgot."

She laughed. "I wish we could forget about it. That would be a whole lot easier."

"But if we go and get it done, then we can go home and forget all about it for now."

And that's what they did. It didn't take very long, and since it was obvious that she was fading quickly, Detective Martin went through it as fast as he could and then said, "Now you better get her home."

"I was planning on it, but then she remembered that whole *stopping on the way home to give you our statements* thing."

"Well, … I appreciate the fact that you did, but now get her home, and enjoy life for a change. That's the Haven doing its job again."

She looked at him and asked, "What job is that?"

He just smiled and didn't say anything. "You'll figure that out over time."

She just smiled and nodded, but it made no sense. When she got back in the vehicle, already exhausted from the rigors of the day, she asked in a tired voice, as they headed back out of town again, "What did he mean?"

"I'm not exactly sure myself, but I think it may be something about matchmaking in the sense of people who are needing a haven to get out of the storm. Then they have a tendency to find each other," he shared.

"Ah." She nodded. "That makes the Haven an even more perfect name, and I really like that connotation."

"Me too," he agreed, patting her knee.

She grabbed his hand with hers and said, "Home, Burke."

He burst out laughing. "Your wish is my command."

He drove as carefully and yet as quickly as he could. As they pulled in, Timber strolled out and walked over to greet them. "How are you doing, Shirley?"

She looked up at him. "Honestly, I'm so ready to go to bed."

"Then get your ass up there," he said, "and no more fighting with bullets on my time, you hear me?"

"Yeah, I wasn't planning on it this time," she noted.

He nodded, then helped her out of the vehicle, as the dogs came running. It was all she could do to calm the dogs down enough to make her way upstairs. As she moved toward her room, Burke was there to help her.

As she crashed on her bed, wincing in pain, he pulled some blankets up over her and whispered, "Get some sleep."

"I'll be very happy to take that advice," she whispered, then almost immediately drifted off.

# CHAPTER 21

B URKE WENT DOWN and helped Timber unload the rest of the groceries and supplies he'd picked up from town. He looked over at him and smiled. "She's tired but doing pretty well now."

"Seems like it, and it appears that you guys turned a corner too."

"I think so," he said, with a smile, "not really a corner I was looking to turn, but …"

Timber nodded and smiled. "You know the turns we take in life that are frequently the best are those we weren't even looking for. And I would say this looks like it's turning out just the way it was always intended to." And, with that, he didn't say any more.

Several days later Burke walked into the dining room to find Shirley standing in front of the whiteboards, glaring at the display. He winced, walked over to the coffeepot, quickly filled his cup, and turned to make his escape, only to find her standing in front of him.

"You're avoiding me," she declared.

He looked at her in surprise and then started to laugh. "Nope, we're all avoiding you."

"Why is that?" she asked in astonishment.

"Because you've been cranky and miserable."

"Yeah, sorry about that," she muttered, wincing. "I just

want to get back to work, and you won't let me."

"Nope, we won't," he agreed, leaning over to give her a big kiss. "Not until you feel better. No work for you, … none at all."

"I'm feeling fine," she snapped. At that, his eyebrows shot up, and she groaned. "Okay, so I'm feeling *better.*"

"*Better* at least is not a lie, but it's not good enough yet."

"Do you see this whiteboard?" she asked in a mutinous tone.

"Yeah, hell, we all see it," he muttered. "That's another reason why we're all avoiding you."

She grinned and then started to laugh.

He pulled up a chair, sat her down gently, and said, "Everything in due time."

"Maybe," she grumbled, "but still, there's a lot of work to be done."

"And we're working on it," he told her. "We're all working on it. You just need time to get back on your feet."

She smiled. "And you're just all enjoying the fact that it'll take me time, aren't you?"

"No, of course not." Then he laughed and added, "Maybe a little bit."

"I'm not trying to rush anybody into doing what they don't want to do," she said in frustration. "I just know that it's easy for all of this to get caught up and then lost in the mess."

"You're doing a great job," he told her.

She sighed. "That did not sound like I'm doing a great job. That sounded like you want me to just let you get up and run."

He burst out laughing, leaned over, gave her a second kiss, longer this time, then added, "Anytime you're feeling better, you just let me know." And, with that, he was gone again.

She groaned in frustration, only to see Toby, with a big grin on his face. She glared at him. "Not you too."

"Hey, you're cranky and miserable, but you're healing," he said, raising his hands, "so we all get that. That's only part of the reason why you're snapping."

Dwight walked past, nodding but staying quiet.

"Burke could do a lot better than me," she muttered.

Dwight stopped, then turned to face her. "I don't think so." And, with that, he walked back into the kitchen and ignored her.

Later that night she decided to talk to Burke, but she wasn't even sure how to do that. It wasn't a conversation she'd ever had to have before. Even if it was needed, it wasn't one that she was terribly comfortable having. But something needed to be done.

When she went up to her room that night, she got ready for bed. Later, as she heard him come upstairs, she waited, then slipped out of her room and over to his. He was still in the act of undressing, sitting down, taking off his prosthetic. He stopped when he saw her, his eyes widening, and she nodded. "You're right. I should have been done with all this."

He frowned.

She shook her head. "I've taken my sweet time, and I'm done with it."

"Okay, done with what though?" he asked cautiously, as he slowly removed his prosthetic leg. She walked over, bent down, and helped him take off the sock covering his stump. She frowned as she saw the scar on the side. "Are you sure you should be working as hard as you are?"

He tapped her on the nose and said, "It's fine."

"Aha, just like I'm fine too. Right?"

He looked at her and started to smile. "Why don't we take care of each other?" he suggested. "Then we won't have to worry about either of us overdoing it."

"I suspect what would *really* end up happening," she replied good-naturedly, "is that we would both end up overdoing it."

He looked at her and smiled. "You could be right."

She leaned over from her kneeling position and kissed him gently. He hesitated, not kissing her back fully. She stroked his cheek and whispered, "Maybe ... you're not ready."

His eyes widened, and he lifted her up by the waist and gently laid her on the bed. She chuckled. "Do you want to wait a little bit?"

"Hell no, but," he began, as he quickly divested himself of his undershirt and to lie down beside her, "I want to confirm you're sure."

"Why don't we both just decide that we're sure and be done with it?" she asked, with a chuckle. "And acknowledge that I'm here because I want to be here."

"That sounds perfect to me. You do know where we're heading, right?" he asked, as he nuzzled her neck and chin.

"Of course," she said.

"No," he leaned back, looked at her, and added, "I'm serious."

"I know," she stated, "and that's why I'm here. I'm serious too."

A warm, gentle smile lit up his face. "Thank you for that."

She shook her head, tapped him on the nose, and added,

"Thank you for just being you."

"You're welcome."

She laughed. "We sound ridiculous."

"No," he argued. "I think it's just part and parcel of us trying to figure out who we are, who we want to be, and who we want to be after that."

"I'm not even sure what that means," she admitted, "but I know that I want to be here and that I want to build a life with you, even if we have no clue where, how, or what that will look like."

"I agree, and I was thinking about that," he shared. "A part of me just wants to stay here at the Haven, but I know Timber can't possibly have any money for wages."

"No, of course not, and he can't handle all of us anyway. Not when you consider that there's Toby and Dwight and Tommy and however many other men are here."

"There is some talk about nearby land being available to buy for building individual houses," he murmured.

She stared at him. "Really?"

He nodded. "Yeah, really."

"Oh." She frowned.

He rolled over, pulled her up against him, careful of her shoulder, and asked, "What does that mean?"

"I just never knew until this moment that it was something that I want rather badly."

"What do you want?" he asked, looking at her.

"A place, a home, like a place of my own, a place where I can rest at the end of a long day," she explained. "I don't even know what that long day looks like, but I already want whatever it is that you're thinking."

He smiled, then leaned over and whispered, "What if we stayed close to here, you know, close to the guys here?"

"That would be perfect," she replied. "They already feel more like family than anything I've ever experienced before."

"That they do," he agreed. "And I guess that's what I'm asking. How do you really feel about building a family close to here?"

"I think it would be perfect," she stated, "and something I've never even thought would be possible."

"It is possible," he declared. "And I would like nothing more."

She smiled. "I think maybe I could handle that myself."

"You think?" he asked, as he kissed her on her chin, then on her cheek, sliding tender kisses across her neck.

She murmured and asked, "Is this really possible for us?"

"It is," he confirmed. "I know you tend to think that nothing good will ever come your way, but you're wrong. Lots of good things are out there for you."

"I'm not sure about that," she countered. "However, plenty of good things are right here for me, and that's the part I still struggle to believe."

"Because you don't realize how very special you are." He leaned down, carefully lowered himself on top of her, and gave her a really deep, soul-searching kiss. "Are you okay?" he asked, when he lifted his head. "Does this hurt your shoulder?"

"You know something?"

"What?"

"I think you talk too much." She pulled him down closer and gave him a deep tongue-lashing kiss all of her own.

By the time they separated to breathe, he added, "You're wearing too many clothes."

"So are you," she added, with a giggle.

They both sat up, stripped off the last of their clothing,

and came together in a flurry of heated skin and wild emotions. By the time they came up for air, she was exhausted and curled up in his arms.

He murmured, "It's nice to know there is still honesty in passion."

"I really don't want you seeing my sister every time you look at me."

"I've never looked at Silvia like this," he declared, "not ever. And she was never someone who looked at me the way you do. She was all about herself. So, don't you ever worry about that. I would never allow thoughts of her to interfere with what I've found with you." He kissed her and vowed, "I promise."

She gave a happy sigh and muttered, "That's good because that would be a ghost I don't want to live with."

"It's no ghost," he stated. "I never for one moment felt about your sister the way I feel about you right now."

She kissed him and whispered, "I'm really glad to hear that. I hate to feel so insecure."

"Your family has made you insecure, but I have a hunch that will gradually take care of itself, as you become happy and content and joyous," he suggested. "One day you will realize that all the other crap has fallen away."

She smiled, gingerly leaned up on her good elbow and added, "You know …"

He waggled his eyebrows. "I do know."

She smiled. "We don't have to get up just yet, do we?"

"Are you kidding? We haven't even slept yet."

"I know. I was kind of hoping maybe we could skip that part."

He burst out laughing and added, "I don't know about skipping that stage completely, since we've got a long day tomorrow, plus you still need extra rest to heal. On the other hand, we could certainly sleep in a bit later than normal." With that, he leaned over and kissed her gently.

"No," she said, "not gentle. I want absolutely everything you have to give." She pulled him down hard on top of her and kissed him with all the need that had been driving her, feeling a release of a pressure that she hadn't even been aware of. Something was driving her, and she realized it was the need to be his, the need to be something special, over and above her sister, and, when he finally entered her, she cried out in joy.

"Easy," he whispered, "take it easy. You don't want to hurt yourself."

"It's fine," she muttered, as she cried out again, "just don't stop, … please. Dear God, don't stop." Very quickly he drove her right up to the edge and then flung her over. She lay panting in his arms, as he climaxed too, then sank down beside her.

She gave a happy sigh. "I don't really think we need two bedrooms, do you?"

"Nope, I sure don't," he agreed. "We can move everything over tomorrow."

"I think Timber was probably wondering about doing it already," she said, with a laugh.

"I wouldn't be at all surprised, but he would never presume."

"I'm sure he could use the space, especially if he really plans to have this be a place for people to come seeking sanctuary. What will he do when he runs out of space?"

"That's why we're all discussing houses."

"You mean, like *soon*, soon?"

"Yeah, really soon. I have some money saved up that

Silvia didn't know about, thankfully, and if we get help building a new home, and it's not a hugely extravagant affair," he muttered, "I think we could probably do one quite nicely."

She looked over at him and nodded. "I have money saved up too, so if we're talking about a house for two, it's probably doable."

He nodded. "Unless you're interested in a house for maybe three or four."

Her eyes widened, and unexpectedly tears came, as she whispered, "Yes, please."

He smiled, pulled her up close, and whispered, "Your wish is my command."

She chuckled and added, "Maybe we need to wait a year."

"That would probably be smart but not much longer." He rolled over, kissed her, and added, "Honestly, I didn't ever expect this to happen."

"Neither did I," she whispered, "but I can't wait for that life to begin." And, with that, she pulled him down for another kiss, knowing in her heart of hearts that, although her sister had made a mess out of things, Shirley was well on her way to the best years of her life.

# EPILOGUE

ABOUT A WEEK later Timber strode up the front yard and watched as the trailer backed up to the paddock. He looked over at Tiffany and asked, "Are you ready for this?"

"No, probably not," she admitted, "but … alpacas and llamas apparently will be part of the family from now on. They are just some of the animals we'll be looking after."

As he walked into the paddock and saw the trailer was full, he smiled because it was either smile or cry, and he was not one to cry very easily, at least not in public. Yet the animals always made him feel such emotions. These animals were horribly thin and desperately in need of shearing and some love and attention.

He looked over at Jimmy, who had driven them here. Timber's tone bleak, he asked, "Is this all of them?"

"It is, and two of them may not even make it," Jimmy warned. "I'm not sure what to say about them."

"No, I don't know either," he murmured, "but let's get going."

At that, another woman walked up.

Timber looked over at her and frowned. "Keisha?"

Keisha nodded. "Hey, Timber. How are you doing?"

"What are you doing here?"

"I heard an extra load of animals was headed this way

when I was talking to Tiffany," she explained, "so I thought I would come lend a hand."

"You're always welcome. You do know Jaxon is here, right?"

She looked over at him and asked, "Is that a problem?"

"Not for me, as long as it's not for you."

"Nope, not a problem for me," she stated. "He's my ex for a reason."

"I know," he replied, "but I also know that it's not an easy ex."

"There's no such thing as easy exes," she declared. She came around to the side and stopped when she saw the animals. "Dear God," she whispered.

"Yeah, I hear you," Tiffany muttered at her side. "Let's get to work."

At that, a shout came from the other side, and Jaxon walked over. "I saw the trailer come in and thought you could use an extra hand. What are we doing?" Then he turned, and his eyes widened when he saw Keisha. "Hey," he muttered, as he pushed back his hat. "I didn't know you would be here."

"I didn't know I would be here either, until I heard so many animals were in need," she shared. "I came to help Tiffany. You got a problem with that?"

As there hadn't been even a hint of a challenge in her tone, everybody else ignored it. Jaxon stared at her, then over at Timber. "No problem here. Animals first."

And, with that, they all got down to work.

This concludes Book 2 of The Haven: Burke.

Read about Jaxon: The Haven, Book 3

# The Haven: Jaxon (Book #3)

Jaxon, regaining his physical health but still haunted by the emotional scars of an unwanted impending divorce, finds solace working at the Haven, where he feels welcomed and at home, at least for now. However, his sense of peace is shattered when Tiffany arranges for the arrival of llamas in distress, and he discovers that Keisha, his ex, is the one transporting them.

Stunned by the encounter, Jaxon struggles to maintain his composure, but his priority remains the animals in need. As he navigates the unexpected tension, he resolves to protect his heart, even if it means being overly cautious. Keisha's sister had been a sore point between them before, and that hadn't changed.

As Jaxon and Keisha begin to communicate and to address their past, a new threat emerges involving her sister, posing unforeseen dangers. Amid the suspense, a heartwarming love starts to rekindle between them, offering hope and healing in the face of adversity.

Find Book 3 here!

To find out more visit Dale Mayer's website.

https://geni.us/DMSTHJaxon

# Author's Note

Thank you for reading Burke: The Haven, Book 2! If you enjoyed the book, please take a moment and leave a short review.

Dear reader,

I love to hear from readers, and you can contact me at my website: www.dalemayer.com or at my Facebook author page. To be informed of new releases and special offers, sign up for my newsletter or follow me on BookBub. And if you are interested in joining Dale Mayer's Reader Group, here is the Facebook sign up page.
http://geni.us/DaleMayerFBGroup

Cheers,
Dale Mayer

# About the Author

Dale Mayer is a *USA Today* best-selling author, best known for her SEALs military romances, her Psychic Visions series, and her Lovely Lethal Garden cozy series. Her contemporary romances are raw and full of passion and emotion (Broken But … Mending, Hathaway House series). Her thrillers will keep you guessing (Kate Morgan, By Death series), and her romantic comedies will keep you giggling (*It's a Dog's Life*, a stand-alone novella; and the Broken Protocols series, starring Charming Marvin, the cat).

Dale honors the stories that come to her—and some of them are crazy, break all the rules and cross multiple genres!

To go with her fiction, she also writes nonfiction in many different fields, with books available on résumé writing, companion gardening, and the US mortgage system. All her books are available in print and ebook format.

## Connect with Dale Mayer Online

*Dale's Website – www.dalemayer.com*
*Twitter – @DaleMayer*
*Facebook Page – geni.us/DaleMayerFBFanPage*
*Facebook Group – geni.us/DaleMayerFBGroup*
*BookBub – geni.us/DaleMayerBookbub*
*Instagram – geni.us/DaleMayerInstagram*
*Goodreads – geni.us/DaleMayerGoodreads*
*Newsletter – geni.us/DaleNews*